BROKEN SOULS

STEPHEN BLACKMOORE

DAW BOOKS, INC.
DONALD A. WOLLHEIM, FOUNDER
375 Hudson Street, New York, NY 10014

ELIZABETH R. WOLLHEIM
SHEILA E. GILBERT
PUBLISHERS
www.dawbooks.com

ACKNOWLEDGMENTS

Books aren't written in a vacuum and this one is no exception. Many thanks to my wife, Kari, whose support knows no bounds, who lets me rail against the world and never tases me, though I'm sure she's thought about it many times. God knows I could have used it.

And I certainly couldn't have done without the insights from Betsy Wollheim, Josh Starr, and the superhero team at DAW, or the occasional talking off a ledge provided by my agent Al Guthrie, who answers all of my stupid questions with a straight face.

Many thanks to the friends who helped shape this story and gave me my very own cheering section. People like Chuck Wendig, John Hornor Jacobs, Chris Holm, Sabrina Ogden, Jaclyn Taylor, LeAnna Bruce, Kristin Sullivan, Brian White, Jeff Macfee, Karina Cooper, the screaming hordes who follow me on Twitter (who are all sexy, sexy people, by the way) and many, many more. I couldn't have done this without them.

But mostly I want to thank you, the reader who

decided to take a chance on my book. You're busy. You have things to do. Thank you for taking the time to read it. I can only hope that it was worth your time and attention and you liked it enough to want to read the next one.

Chapter 1

There are a lot of ghosts in Los Angeles. Haunts stare out from the doorways they died in, Wanderers blindly mingle with street hustlers, neither knowing of the other's presence. Echoes stutter their way through their final moments, broken records skipping over and over and over again until they finally fade away.

There are other kinds of ghosts. Torn-down landmarks, faded histories, memories of things you'll never get back. You can see hints of them. Tiny slivers in the faded California bungalows, the churches on Adams, the brownstones in an increasingly gentrified Skid Row. L.A.'s a ghostly city whose heyday was marked by illusions, corruption and broken dreams. They'll all fade away eventually, too. Bulldozed over for a Metro line, a mixed-use complex of shops and condos, a parking lot.

And then there are the ghosts you can't get rid of, no matter how hard you try.

I sit in my car, the latest in a series of stolen vehicles,

and look up at Vivian's condo on Wilshire. Lights are off, as I expected. Two in the morning, after all. I haven't been here in a few weeks. I check in on her every once in a while, though if she knew she'd probably shoot me. She made it abundantly clear that I'm at the top of her shit list about six months ago at Alex's funeral. Rightly so.

She and I had been dating since high school when I left L.A. fifteen years ago. Hell of a way to break up with a person. I didn't even leave a note. So of course she and my best friend were going to hook up. Hell, when I came back to town, she and Alex were about to move in with each other. They spent all that time building a life together, taking on responsibilities that should have been mine. Playing siblings to my younger sister.

To be fair, I didn't leave by choice. Got one of those 'offers you can't refuse' deals. Leave L.A. Don't come back. Or we kill you, your sister, your friends, your dog, your third grade math teacher. You get the idea.

So, you know, I left.

I glance across the street and get a flash of memory and a stabbing headache. Walking down to a movie in Westwood about five years ago, girl on my arm, slightly drunk. Only I wasn't in L.A. five years ago. The memory isn't mine.

A while back I consumed a ghost. Something I didn't know I could do. Real bastard by the name of Jean Boudreau, who I thought I'd taken out fifteen years ago. Tore him to pieces, swallowed him up.

Bad enough to have chunks of his memories floating around my head. Worse is that he'd been doing the same to other ghosts. Thousands of them, decades of memories he'd consumed, pulled into himself. All those broken ghosts swallowed up to patch the holes in his own decaying soul.

I'd get these sudden flashes. Little things mostly, but vivid. Remembering something I never did. A person I'd never met, a meal I'd never eaten. Sometimes the memories would swallow everything up. I'd forget where I was, who I was. The worst lasted three days and I came to shaking and naked in a burnt-out cabin in the Mojave.

This is what happens when you eat other people's souls. I don't recommend it.

The headache fades along with the memory of the date I never had and I let out a breath I hadn't realized I'd been holding. The episodes have gotten less frequent, less vivid. I don't wake up in the middle of the night speaking a foreign language and wondering where I am anymore. But they still hit me from time to time, and I never know when I'm going to get a bad one.

My phone, a burner I picked up at a grocery store, buzzes in the car's cup holder. Text message. "GRIFFITH OBSERVATORY."

Odd choice, but okay. I'm not the one calling the shots here. I put the car in gear, pull away from the curb. Wonder if I'll ever be able to fix things. Wonder if they're meant to stay broken.

———

When you finally get a meeting with the guy who can help you unfuck your life, you say yes, no matter how weird the place he wants to meet you might be. Maybe he's testing you, maybe he's showing off. Don't know, don't care.

I pull into the empty hilltop parking lot of the Griffith Observatory, the three-domed building perched on the edge of Griffith Park overlooking the neighborhood of Los Feliz. Two in the morning. There's no one here. The park's closed, patrolled by rangers in SUVs who, with a little magical assistance, drive by me oblivious as I wind my way up the hill. I park the stolen Mercedes right at the edge of the lawn. At the other end of the lot sits a white Bentley.

Harvey Kettleman is kind of a mage's mage. More research than practice, but he's well known among the magic set and big in L.A. If you're a talent of any standing in this city you've heard of him. I first met Kettleman about twenty years ago. My dad and he weren't tight, exactly. Seems mages get to a certain point and they never really trust anybody. We have associations of convenience more than we have real friendships. Magic is power, and power does that to a person.

I hope he doesn't remember I called him Gandalf when I was a kid.

So I went through a third party. Guy I know in Torrance named Jack MacFee. Two-bit hustler mostly. Purveyor of the trappings of magic, the things we need to ply our craft. Goat's blood, graveyard dirt, ground up bone from convicted murderers, that sort of thing. Stuff you can't grab at your local Target.

Took a while, but MacFee finally came through. Owes me from way back and I owe him. We stopped chalking up the favors years ago. Seeing him was one of the few bright spots in coming back to this shithole town.

I can see Kettleman on the roof-deck of the Observatory, silhouetted against an amber haze. Clouds have moved in and the streetlights of L.A. cast the sky a sickening, nighttime yellow. I'm not expecting trouble, but then that's when it usually gets me. I slide my Browning Hi-Power into the holster at the small of my back. It's an old Nazi pistol with so much hate embedded in its frame that holding it feels like cockroaches under my fingers. It's a weird gun and an ugly gun. All its nightmare history sings to my magic, and when I pull that trigger it'll punch through shit like a .44.

I slip my pocket watch, an Illinois Sangamo Special from 1919 with a wicked way of twisting time, into my coat pocket. I haven't used it in months. It's iffy at the best of times and horrifying at the worst. I have no idea where it came from, only that it's been in my family for a couple generations. I wonder sometimes if maybe it has a mind of its own.

Neither the gun nor the watch is something I want to use, but better to have them and not need them than the other way around. I head across the grass past the parking lot and up the stairs on the side of the building that holds the observatory's seventy-year-old telescopes.

When I'm halfway up, a disturbingly familiar voice at my ear says, "He's going to try to kill you," and I freeze.

Is this another episode? It doesn't feel like one.

Those are memories, not voices, and the stabbing headache that hits with them isn't there. I look behind me, but don't see anyone nearby. My sense of the Dead tells me the same thing. No ghosts on the stairs. I cast my net a little wider, stretch my senses. A few ghosts of dead hobos down the hill, some guy who got shot on a nearby trail. There is something weird, though. A ghost I can't identify, flittering on the edge of my awareness, there one second, gone the next. I almost don't catch it.

That's strange. If there's a ghost around I'll know it. Whether I want to or not. This thing is bouncing in and out of my awareness like a radio signal in the desert. Like nothing I've run into before. But the really strange part?

It's up on the roof with Kettleman.

———

"Evening, Mr. Kettleman," I say, coming around the western telescope dome, its green copper plating gray in the hazy light. "Unusual place for a meeting, isn't it?" He's standing by the central dome looking up at the night sky, wearing a dark blue suit and a gray overcoat, a neatly trimmed beard and shaved head giving him a professorial look. The ghost I can feel up here is still around, closer, but just as hard to pinpoint. I can feel traces of it, but not the whole thing. Like seeing shattered glass and knowing it's a bottle from the shards.

"Eric Carter," he says. "Yes, I suppose, but I always like a bit of gravitas to these sorts of things. Your father used to give me such grief over it, you know." He's thinner than I remember. Older, his beard grayer. Stands to reason. I haven't seen him since I was a kid.

"Yes, sir," I say. There's something wrong here. His voice is stilted, like he's not used to using the words.

"It's been a long time, young man," he says. He cocks his head to the side like he's trying to remember something. "Gandalf."

I was afraid of that. "That was a long time ago, too, sir. I've been out of town some years. Only been back a few months."

"I heard," he says. "My condolences on your family. Then and now. I was at your parents' funeral, though I'm afraid I only learned about your sister recently. I'm very sorry for your loss."

After my parents died I went off the reservation and killed the mage who murdered them. That's when his assistant, Ben Griffin, gave me the choice to get out of town or die along with my sister and all my friends. Kept me off of this coast for a long time. Until a few months ago, when my sister was murdered and all bets were off.

"Thank you. I hear the services were very tasteful."

"No amount of ceremony can dull the bite that death comes for us all. But then no one knows that better than you, eh? How is the necromancy business these days?"

"Kinda dead," I say, the old joke coming out before I can catch myself. "It's actually what I'm here to talk to you about," I say.

"Yes. I understand you have a problem with a death goddess," he says. "Mictecacihuatl. Santa Muerte, herself. She's a nasty one. You should have come to me sooner."

"With all due respect, sir, I tried. You weren't exactly picking up my calls."

He waves away the sarcasm. "I have no time for the uncommitted. I needed to make sure you wanted to see me badly enough. Mister MacFee was very persuasive on your behalf. So you have my attention. I suppose you're looking for a way to rid yourself of her influence?"

"That's the hope. I know it's a long shot, but anything that might help sever my link to her would be appreciated."

He frowns. "You know there are others who can help you. There's a man I know in London who—"

"I need to stay in town, sir."

"Oh?"

"Personal reasons." I don't need to tell him everything. Keeping tabs on Vivian is my business.

"I see. Well, then let's see what we're up against, shall we? Come here. Let me look at your eyes." He turns to me, tugging at the corner of his own eye, like he's trying to put something back in place. He twitches as he does it. Nervous tic?

The voice I heard on the stairs pipes up. "Watch yourself," it says. It's clearer this time. It takes all I have not to spin around and ask who's there, even though I know that voice. I know who it belongs to. And I know it's not possible. It's not the broken ghost hiding up here on the roof, that much I'm sure of. Probably just my paranoia. A new psychosis, maybe. Wouldn't that be fun?

At night from a distance it's easier to pass my eyes

off as normal. I step closer, but not too close. Give him a good look.

"Oh my," he says. "No iris. No whites at all. Pitch black. Did it hurt?"

"Wasn't pleasant."

"And now?"

"No. Seem to have slightly better night vision, but they don't give me trouble in bright light, either. Been wearing sunglasses a lot so I don't scare the straights."

"And I heard mention of a ring?"

I show him my left hand, the wedding band on my finger. It changes from time to time. A simple gold band sometimes, tiny *calaveras* carved into its surface others. Tonight it's solid green jade, which is new. "Came with the eyes," I say. "Can't seem to get rid of that, either."

The ring and the eyes are reminders from Santa Muerte that I belong to her now. I made a deal with her, to help me kill Boudreau after he'd kidnapped Alex, but I ended up with a shotgun wedding and Alex dead instead. Pro tip: read the fine print.

"Interesting," he says. "Married to a goddess of death. Are you sure you want me to help you break her hold on you? I imagine you must be getting some benefits from this arrangement."

Sure. I've got more power. My abilities to sense the dead have skyrocketed. I can channel more magic than I've ever been able to before. I can cast some spells that used to take me days of planning with barely a thought. But there's more to this than all that.

"She wants something from me and I don't know what. Can't be anything good."

"But the power—"

"You don't get it. This isn't about power. It's about being somebody's puppet. Yeah, my abilities have grown, but I don't own them. Can you help me or not?"

He looks set to argue with me about it, then catches himself. "I see. All right. Has she contacted you since this happened?"

I remember Alex's funeral when she came to gloat. The same day Vivian told me to stay out of her life. "Just once. Few months back. Haven't seen her since."

"Interesting." He cocks his head to the side, wrinkles his brow in thought. "Here, give me your hand. I have something that might help until we can find something more permanent." He reaches into his coat pocket.

Something's not right. "Sure you don't need to know a little more about this?"

"No, no," he says, a hungry look creeping into his eyes. "I know enough. Now, come here." I'm not buying it.

"He's got a knife," the voice in my ear says, as if confirming my suspicions.

Sure enough, Kettleman whips out a wicked-looking blade made of knapped obsidian, its handle just a wrapping of old leather strands covering the stone. He slashes it out at me in a wide arc, faster than I expected. It bites through my suit coat, nicks my tie.

I call my magic around me, shove a burst of lightning out through my hand. Two months ago, channeling this much power would have made me pull from the local pool and probably left me exhausted, but now the magic flows through me fast and smooth. The arcs of electricity dance around Kettleman, but he's no slouch. They bounce off a shield he's put up around himself, and the force of my blast only manages to shove him back a couple feet. He grunts against the onslaught and then lets out his own.

A wave of force smashes into me. Knocks me down and I skid ten feet to slam against the concrete wall of the western telescope dome. Wasn't ready for that.

"The power of a goddess," Kettleman says, advancing on me like a madman, the obsidian blade flashing in his hand. "You don't want it, you don't deserve to keep it."

"Jesus, man, it's not like I can give it to ya. Hell, if that's all it took I'd hand it over right now." I roll to my feet, draw the Browning from its holster at the small of my back. "Look, I don't want to kill you. Really. Getting this far was a pain in the ass and I'm not in the mood to start over."

His eyes narrow into slits, his hand tightens on the obsidian blade. "You're not worthy of the gift," he says. "You don't know what to do with it. It belongs with someone who does. I'll skin you alive and wear you like a suit."

There's an image I didn't need. "Don't think it really works that way."

The floor shudders, a sound of twisting metal behind me. I've been so focused on him I hadn't realized he was setting something up behind me. A long strip of the copper sheeting covering the telescope's dome tears off and whips down at me. I roll out of the way as it strikes where I was standing. Sparks fly.

Kettleman is on me in a flash. I block his swing with my forearm, drive my palm into his face. I give the strike some magical oomph and hear a loud crack as his nose crunches. He wails in pain, stumbles back, blood streaming from his nose. I could probably end this here. Keep hammering him in the face until he goes down and stays down. But that could kill him. Psycho or not, I need him.

Instead I bolt for the other side of the building. There's another staircase I can take down. If I can get away from the crazy I can regroup. I've spent too much time trying to get a lead on how to get out from under Santa Muerte's thumb. There's got to be some way to reason with him. But to do that I need to get him to quit trying to turn me into a pair of pants. I round the curve of the other telescope and skid to a stop.

I've found that ghost. The one that kept flitting in and out like a bad radio station. It's definitely not the one who warned me of the attack. This one's in no shape to communicate at all. It flickers in and out worse than any ghost I've ever seen. Disjointed, scattered. It stands there, its face a sick imitation of Munch's scream, its body a parody of cohesion. It looks sliced crosswise like a man trapped in a mix-and-match puzzle book for kids where the top and bottom pieces don't quite line up. I've never seen a ghost this incoherent. Even if it were old and faded it wouldn't be like this. This thing is broken.

But it's worse than that. The ghost is Kettleman's.

Unless the old mage has a twin who just happened to die on this rooftop, this is him. Every last detail is there. Same face, same suit, same salt-and-pepper goatee. But if this is Kettleman's ghost, who's the maniac with the knife?

Before I get a chance to really put any thought into it I hear that warning voice in my ear say, "Duck." I don't argue, just drop down and let Not-Kettleman's knife sail over my head. I lash back with my leg, catching him above the knee. He screams as the joint pops and he stumbles. The knife falls from his hand. I kick it out of the way.

If this isn't the real Kettleman then there's no reason to hold back. I bring the Browning to bear but I underestimate his speed. His good leg sweeps up in a vicious kick with a healthy dose of magic behind it and slams into my forearm. My entire arm goes numb as the gun flies out of my hand and skitters away from me.

So I change tactics and kick him in the nuts. His scream goes up an octave and he starts to make retching noises. I've been dealing with this Santa Muerte bullshit for too long and Kettleman was the closest thing to a lead I had. God fucking dammit.

"Why'd you have to go and kill him, you sonofabitch? And who the hell are you?" I slam the heel of my foot into his crotch a couple more times, letting adrenaline, anger and frustration fuel every blow.

When I get done with this bastard there's not going to be anything left beyond a smear. I step up to curb stomp his skull, bring my leg up and—

He's not Kettleman anymore. There's a tearing noise as the guy he's turned into rips through his clothes. They're way too small for him. He's a foot taller at least, and packing more muscle than half a dozen juiced up linebackers. Crew-cut blond hair, clean-shaven, thick cords of muscle, Cyrillic tattoos across his chest. There's blood still on his face but there's no sign of the broken nose I just gave him, or the busted knee. That can't be a good sign.

He reaches up with both hands, grabs my foot mid-stomp and yanks me onto my ass. I land on the hard concrete and the air punches out of me, my vision blurs. I reach into my coat pocket, struggle for a breath. Not-Kettleman, now a good fit for an extra in a Russian prison movie, pulls himself up off the floor. He reaches down, yanks me up, cocks back his sledgehammer fist.

That's when I get hold of the pocket watch, twist the crown with my thumb and push the button. I don't have a lot of control over the watch. I can aim its time-twisting effect, but that's about it. Like most magic it's more like a negotiation than an actual command. I want this fucker over and done with. Tacking forty or fifty decades onto him ought to do it.

As usual, the watch has its own ideas. Not-Kettleman screams, drops me and stumbles back, but I don't see any noticeable difference. No wrinkles, liver spots, anything like that. What did it hit him with? A day? A week? I can't tell, but even a few minutes ought to hurt like a sonofabitch.

I get the watch all the way out of my pocket, air slowly coming back into my lungs. He's backing away now, real fear on his face. I spin the crown a couple more times with my thumb. Let's see how he likes another hit from the watch.

I half expect him to rush me, but instead he runs to the fallen knife, grabs it and shifts back to his Kettleman form. There's no flash, no pop, no downsizing of Hulk rage. He's just a skinny academic beat to shit with a flattened nose and a busted knee. No help there, it seems. But I guess he doesn't need much. He jumps off the roof.

I hit the watch button again, but I have to see him for it to do much. Instead the concrete of the wall he's jumped over blisters, a hundred years of wear pitting its surface. I look at the watch. Now you work? I crawl to the wall and look over the side. Not-Kettleman has gone back into Russian mobster mode, barely a scratch on him. Nice strategy. Use the Kettleman form to take the brunt of the fall and then saunter away.

I bring up the watch for another shot, but he's too far away. Dry firing it isn't recommended. If it can't hit the target I want it'll hit something else and there's no telling what kind of mess that'll cause. I watch him get behind the wheel of the Bentley, gun the engine and tear out of the parking lot.

With the fight over my hands start shaking from the dump of adrenaline. What the fuck just happened?

"Told you he'd try to kill you," says the voice in my ear, cutting through the sound of the revving engine, the screeching tires.

"Yeah," I say. "You want to tell me what this is about? You real? Or am I just going insane?"

If it has an answer, the voice keeps it to itself. Just as well. I don't think I could handle hearing the truth. I know that voice, know its inflections, I know the sort of thing it might say. It's a voice I'm very familiar with. I just haven't heard in a while.

It's the voice of Alex, the friend I couldn't save, the one whose soul was chewed up by a ghost I couldn't destroy fast enough. I'm not stupid enough to think he couldn't come back from that. I've seen it happen before. But if he's a ghost I should feel it. Not just get this disembodied voice in my head. And if he is back, I'm not sure if I should be glad or worried.

After all, I'm the one who put a bullet in his head.

Chapter 2

The memory of Alex's voice rings in my mind, but I push it out. That's a question for later. Right now I need to see what I can find out about what the hell just happened. I could try chasing the Not-Kettleman, but what's the point? By the time I get to the car he'll be halfway down the hill. Besides, I don't need the fake when I have the real one right here.

I limp over to where I saw Kettleman's ghost. It's still going in and out of my perception like static. I'm really having a hard time putting my finger on what's wrong with it. It's too disjointed for a Haunt or a Wanderer, and it doesn't have the looped recording feel of an Echo. It just feels . . . incomplete.

I can't see it, which isn't too unusual. Sometimes ghosts are just too old and faded and seeing them is a challenge, other times they like to hide. That's what this one has done, probably freaked out by the fight I just had with its killer. Ghosts can hide from my sight if they want to, and if they're aware enough to even notice I'm around. Fade from view or just dissolve into a building, sink into the ground. Haunts, ghosts tied to a particular location, tend to be more bashful than Wanderers, the ghosts that aren't locked to a specific place. Never understood why. Probably because the Wanderers can just up and leave if they don't like the look of you.

I don't know when the next park ranger patrol will be coming by the Observatory, or what happened to the guards that should already be here, so I don't want to linger too long, but I need answers and I might not get a chance to come back anytime soon. I focus my will at the ghost I know is up here to bring it out. Before I got linked to Santa Muerte this took a lot of effort, not to mention a fair amount of my own blood, but now I can do it with just a thought.

And nothing happens. I try it again, pushing out more forcefully with my will. And still nothing happens. Huh. That hasn't happened in months. There's definitely something wrong with this ghost.

"Fine, you want to play it that way?" I roll up the left sleeve of my coat and shirt, pull out the straight razor I keep in my coat pocket. The tattoos that cover my body from neck to wrists to ankles have a small, scarred gap on the inside of my left forearm.

Most magic is an act of pure willpower, a negotiation with reality. Any decent mage can toss off a small spell, and sometimes even a big one, without much more than thought. But some magic is steeped in ritual, follows laws laid down when humans were still setting fires with sticks. It demands payment.

I nick my forearm with the razor, let a few drops of blood spill on the concrete, focus my will again to make it appear. A hundred Wanderers in a mile-wide area start to rush in with the sound of a jet engine that only I can hear, the roof of the Observatory filling up like the Staples Center at a Lakers game. Their forms overlap, flow in and out of each other in a seething mess of limbs and faces.

They all scream for a taste of that blood, a howling, nightmare chorus. They want to suck the life out of it, hoping for a little bit of life to hang onto. They're desperate for it, and though I've done this thousands of times if I'm not careful they'll kill me. After all, the blood's just an appetizer. I'm the main course.

I push them back with my will, make a bubble for the one I want. They hover over the observatory, hammer against its walls. Sorry, folks, this is an exclusive party and you're not invited.

Kettleman's ghost stutters into view, fading in and out, but reasonably solid. It's wild-eyed, confused. It whips its head back and forth, panic writ large on its face. The weird split of its body, as though it were sliced into chunks and badly stitched together, moves out of sync with itself.

"The hell happened to you?" It startles at my voice, looks at me, blinks. "Come on, you can do it," I say, trying to coax an answer from it. It opens its mouth, stammers a bit. Lets loose an earsplitting scream.

The sound punches through my skull like an ice pick, sending me to my knees. I slam my will down on Kettleman's ghost, send it back to whatever slice of the afterlife it was hiding behind before I bled to call it out, cutting it off midshriek. The sound rings in my ears as a high-pitched whine and I can feel a migraine forming behind my eyes. Okay, so that didn't go as planned.

The ghosts are rushing in now that my concentration is shot. They can't take the blood without permission. Not from where they're standing. There's a barrier between us and unless I give them the go-ahead to go after the blood all they can do is beg.

"Knock yourself out," I say and the ghosts all converge on the few tiny drops on the concrete, their forms all flowing together as they try to get a taste.

I pull myself to my feet, my head ringing from Kettleman's shriek. Seriously, that felt like it punched through my goddamn soul. I doubt his ghost is going anywhere soon, though it's hard to say with the condition it's in. Ghosts fade over time, no matter what type they are, some just take longer than others. I'm a pretty good judge of how long one will last, but with him I honestly have no clue. Could be a day, could be a hundred years. Regardless, if I want to actually talk to it I think I'm going to need to get some more safeguards. I'll catch him later when I'm more prepped.

I head down the stairs opposite the side I came up. When I get near the bottom I see splotches on the steps. With the yellowed night sky washing everything out I can't tell what color they are, but I can guess. I pull out my cell phone and shine the light onto one of them.

Yeah, that's blood, all right. I take a few steps further, following the trail. He dripped a lot at the bottom, like he stopped bleeding about ten steps up. Interesting.

When I get to the bottom the smell hits me. When a person dies they let out a lot of stuff, and not just blood. It only takes me a second to find the corpse hastily dumped into the bushes near the stairs. I kneel down to get a closer look.

I'm willing to bet it's Kettleman's corpse, but I can't be entirely sure. It's just one massive wound, completely skinned. Nothing but raw muscle lying in a pool of blood, piss and shit. Blank, lidless eyes stare up at me like an accusation.

Puts a little more perspective on the crazy fucker upstairs. What was it he said? I'll skin you alive and wear you like a suit? Guess he meant it.

This kind of work takes time. Take him out, skin him, do whatever mojo to take his form. No idea how long that magic would take. But the skinning? That shit should take hours, right? So Kettleman had to have been here long before I showed up. Makes sense that he would have gotten here early to make sure he had the upper hand on me in case I tried something funny. Guess he wasn't paranoid enough, though.

This kind of preparation has me wondering who the target was here. Was it just Kettleman and I happened to be in the way, or was the guy after me? Hell, maybe he wanted both of us. And how did he find out? Did somebody tip him off? Did he take the skin of someone Kettleman knew and get the information that way? How did he even sneak up on him? If he looked like someone Kettleman trusted, that might do it. Get close enough and then shank him with that knife he tried to use on me. A lot of questions are bouncing around my head right now and I only know one thing for sure.

This guy's an idiot.

I flip open my phone, take a few snapshots of the corpse from various angles. Then I dial 911. "Apologies for this stunning breach of etiquette," I say to the corpse as the phone rings. Getting the police involved in mage business is a dick move, but sometimes they can be useful.

Emergency services have gotten worse in L.A. since I was here last. I stay on the phone for almost ten minutes before a woman comes on the line saying, "911, what is your emergency?"

"Hey, I'm up at Griffith Park by the observatory and there's a dead guy up here. Completely skinned. Real mess. Lying next to the front door of the observatory."

"Sir, is this a joke?" I probably sound too calm for what I'm telling her.

If the Not-Kettleman was smart, he'd have dumped the body in the trunk, stepped into Kettleman's life. Who knows how long he could have kept that up without anyone noticing. But with the corpse sitting here, he's just screwed himself out of that.

"You can tell where I'm calling from, right? Some GPS thing? Then you know I'm at the observatory. You're probably going to need dental records or something, because seriously, the guy's got no skin left. His name is Harvey Kettleman. I don't know where he lives. You'll figure that out. Oh, and if you talk to him it might not really be him. Just so you know."

"I'm sorry?"

"Not half as much as I am, lady." I hang up the phone. I delete the history, though I'm sure they can pull it out of the phone, anyway. That's fine. It's a burner and the only numbers I've called on this are MacFee and the nice lady at 911. MacFee'll be pissed, but come on, if he can't get out of a couple uncomfortable conversations with the police then the guy shouldn't be in a business where he routinely sells body parts.

I wipe the phone down on my coat, check it for stray hair, fingerprints and all that, and dump it in the bushes a couple feet from the corpse. Even if the Not-Kettleman comes back to grab the body before the police do at least there will be some evidence for them to grab onto. It's not like they'll catch the guy or lock him up, but it'll cause him some hassle and word will get to the rest of the mages in town. The more people who know Kettleman's dead, the better.

Might help keep some of them alive.

———

We are creatures of habit. Like it or not we fall into ruts, wear our preferences like comfortable shoes. Even when we know we're doing it we're drawn to those things whether they're useful to us or not.

I pull into the parking lot of the Westbourne Inn, a fifties-era motel in need of a major overhaul off of Pass Avenue in Burbank. Googie lettering on a faded plastic sign in front of the building declares Color TV, Reasonable Rates and Checkout at Noon.

But it says nothing about the ghosts.

I'm drawn to these places the way the ghosts are drawn to me. Rundown and out of the way, forgotten and forlorn. Temporary ports in a storm. Hard to chalk this one up to temporary. Been here a month now. Longest stint in any place since I left home in the nineties. Well, I did spend a couple years in jail, but that was by choice. I was learning some things from the ghost of another necromancer in a cell in Arizona. Long story.

I keep telling myself I'm only in L.A. to get shit sorted out, get out from under that sword Santa Muerte's got hanging over me. But I think it's time I own up to the fact that that's all bullshit. I'm still here because if I don't dance to Santa Muerte's tune I'm going to lose more than just Alex.

When I saw Santa Muerte last at Alex's funeral we left things at an impasse. Sure I can fuck with her plans if I absolutely have to, whatever the hell they might be, but that just puts the people I care about in her sights. People like Vivian.

If she tries anything to hurt Viv, at least if I'm in L.A. I'm close enough to deal with it. Last time I was gone, Santa Muerte murdered my sister to get this whole ball rolling. I won't let her do that again.

Ideally, I'd kill Santa Muerte, but I haven't figured out how to crack that particular nut, yet. How do you kill a death goddess? That was part of what I was hoping to get from Kettleman.

The ghosts of the Westbourne Inn flit in and out of my vision as I walk to my room, their passing on the other side invisible to everyone but me. Some of them notice me, most don't. A cluster of them hang out by my door, stopped by the palindromes I've carved into the doorjamb, counting the sunflower seeds I left on the doorstep.

Those alone will keep them out, and I have more powerful wards scrawled on the room's walls in ink I've mixed with goat's blood and ground-up bone that I got from a local *carniceria*. Between those and the psychic camouflage the presence of so many ghosts gives me I'm not too worried about being caught unaware if anything nasty decides to come calling. If anything's coming into this room it's because I let it in the door.

The Westbourne's surprisingly full, at least of the Dead. Haunts and Wanderers left over from the motel's heyday in the fifties. Starlets who missed their big break, washed out second-string actors, men and women trying to get in the door at the nearby Warner Brothers lot and never quite making it. An unsurprising number of them are suicides. Then there are the usual overdosed addicts, beaten prostitutes, a couple dead johns who had coronaries doing the nasty on a Saturday night.

The motel still has a thriving late night business and makes most of its money on an hourly basis. Fine by me. I don't bother the locals, they don't bother me. Sure, the place is a rathole, but that just makes it easier to leave when I need to pick up stakes.

I close the door on the yammering ghosts outside. The room is pretty standard for this sort of place. The sheets are clean, at least, and I have a couple spells that help with the cockroaches.

I leaf through a book from a stack on the floor. Mostly folklore and archeological textbooks about Meso-American gods. Brundage's *Fifth Sun*, Townsend's *Aztecs*, looking for anything that might give me an idea of what Muerte wants from me. Dry reading, to say the least. I haven't been able to finish any of them without nodding off. I've scoured websites from a computer at the library. Trawled through online forums. All useless.

Case in point, before she got her hooks into me Santa Muerte already had a husband, Mictlantecuhtli. King of Mictlan. Ruled by her side. According to an ex-friend of mine who's been around long enough to know, Mictlantecuhtli killed himself after the Spanish invaded the New World, which is something I didn't know gods could do. That's not something you're going to find in a textbook.

I hang up my jacket, inspect it for cuts. There are a few spots I didn't notice before where the Not-Kettleman tagged me with that knife. The fuck is up with that thing, anyway?

I have an idea where to start looking for that, but not until daylight. I need to at least get a couple hours' sleep before I fall over. But that doesn't mean my brain isn't working overtime trying to figure out the other weird thing from the evening. Alex's voice.

I'd like to think I'm not hallucinating. For normal people, when their dead friends start talking to them it's because they're having a psychotic break. But when it happens to a guy who sees ghosts for a living it's just par for the course. Unless there's no ghost there.

And that's the problem. Alex was dead before I put

a bullet in his head. That ghost I ate, Jean Boudreau, had taken up residence in Alex's body and chowed down on his soul.

No soul, no ghost. It's not like I haven't been wrong about that before, of course. I thought I had destroyed Boudreau's soul, too, fifteen years ago, only to have it come back stronger than before.

But this doesn't feel the same. When I finally ran into Boudreau I knew it. I could feel him as a ghost. An unusual one, sure, one who broke the rules as I knew them, but still a ghost. Around spirits I get a feeling like I'm being watched, only with Boudreau it was cranked up to eleven.

I get a thought I like even less. Could this be Alex in my head? With all of the other ghosts Boudreau had consumed, did I get him, too? I'm pretty sure that when Boudreau consumed him he destroyed him completely. Of all the bits of memory I got from Boudreau and the ghosts he built himself up with, none of them seem to have been Alex's. I've never had flashes of his memories like I've had with the other episodes. And if I were going to start talking to any of the ghosts I'd consumed, I would expect it to be Boudreau.

So, if I break it down, my options appear to be Alex is back, but he's not a ghost. Or I'm going crazy. Awesome.

Let's put aside the crazy idea for a second. If Alex isn't a ghost then what the hell is he? There aren't a lot of options for an unmoored soul. It's pretty much ghost or gone. I pace the room, feel the buzz of the ghosts on the other side of the door, hovering in the other rooms.

Maybe I'm looking at it wrong. Assumptions have fucked me before. Thinking something isn't possible didn't do me any favors the last time. So let's assume that he's back as . . . something. If that's true then maybe I'm not the only one he's tried to contact. I got the guy killed, I can't imagine I'm at the top of his list of folks to hang out with. But I can think of a couple people who might be.

The obvious one is Vivian. They were going to move in together. Hell, they were probably going to get married one day. That would make her a hell of a lot more important to him than me. I consider tracking her down and ditch the idea. I know she won't talk to me.

But there's Tabitha. Waitress at Alex's bar. Turned into an apprentice of sorts. Found out she was a talent and he started training her in how to use her magic.

Of course, talking to her has its own pitfalls. We had a bit of a thing for a while. Hardly more than a first date, really. Then the shit hit the fan and I haven't spoken to her since. For the first couple of weeks after Alex died she called or texted me every day, but I never picked up, deleted all her messages without listening to them. Then I threw the phone away. Do I know how to burn a bridge, or what?

I doubt she'll be happy to see me, but I don't really know how angry she'll be. I do have a pretty good idea of how pissed off Vivian is, though, so in this case Tabitha's a better bet. But first I have to have a conversation with MacFee, and that's not happening until the morning.

Chapter 3

Every city has a Shadow Market, those places you go to buy things Walmart's never going to carry. Luck charms that really work, low-grade curses that'll give your enemies warts or a bad case of the clap, protections and wards for all and sundry.

Some of the markets are hidden. Some are out in the open. New York's got five, from the one in an abandoned subway tunnel that hasn't seen a train in a hundred years, to the group-run stoop sale spread across half a dozen brownstones in Brooklyn.

New Orleans' sits within Metairie Cemetery in waterlogged passageways shored up by two-hundred-year-old lumber with an entrance through a Confederate soldier's mausoleum. One in Downtown L.A. is hidden in plain sight, selling love potions and bullet-ward charms alongside the Skid Row hustlers selling knock-off Prada and Louis Vuitton. Whether it's a collection of street vendors selling from blankets out in the open or a hidden complex in an abandoned sewer, every city's got one.

Used to be a drive-in movie theater down in Torrance. You know, back when everything was drive-in; A&W stands, Tiny Naylors' car-hop diner, Bob's Big Boy in Burbank. Big lot, huge screen. Cram five kids under a blanket in the back of your van to see some Disney flick for a buck.

Then in the eighties, they fell apart. No money in drive-in movies with tinny car speakers when you've got a metroplex down at the local mall. So it closed down as a drive-in but opened up as a neverending swap meet.

It's the perfect cover. So many people selling so much crap the normals never suspect some of it's magic. If you know what you're looking for, usually a variant on an old hobo sign for somebody who fences stolen goods, a hook on its side with a line through it, you'll find them.

Most of the stalls are full of crap. Luggage, clothes, computers, cookware, rugs, food, bootleg DVDs, sex toys, knockoff iPods. You want it, somebody's got it. Probably break on you inside of a week, of course. The magic gear is a lot more reliable. Has to be. You sell some kid a busted iPad that's one thing, you sell a mage hemlock that turns out to be salad greens you might not live very long.

I thought about setting up shop here myself when I was a kid. Seemed like a good gig. Somebody's always trying to talk to their dead grandmother or their murdered husband. When you can get them to talk, ghosts have a lot to say, though most of it's just bitching about the life they don't have anymore. But then the shit hit the fan and I took that show on the road instead.

I recognize a few of the vendors moving magical crap from when I used to come here as a kid. Amazing that they're still in business. I pass a stall run by an old Vietnamese woman, face burnt brown, carved with deep wrinkles like she's made out of wood. She's selling thimble-sized caps of liquid magic alongside bootleg USB drives and knockoff computer parts. Wouldn't know it to look at them, though. They've got some minor do-not-touch charms on them. I doubt the normals even know they're there.

The liquid in the thimbles is something to give you a little extra oomph when you need it. Pricey stuff, but for some mages it's the only way to go. Not everyone who can cast can generate much power on their own. That's where the local magic well comes in. Shit's like the Force. Surrounds everything, permeates everything. There's no light side or dark side. That's like calling electricity good or evil. It just is.

I pick up one of the caps, the stall's proprietor watching me carefully. Roll it around my fingers, get a sense for it. Magic doesn't have a taste or a smell, exactly, but that's what it feels like. It changes from place to place, season to season. New York is heavy like hammers and brass. San Francisco is ornate and complicated. L.A. is all over the map.

The stuff in the cap's got the sewage stink of industrial waste, the rancid tang of malt liquor.

"Wilmington?" I say, thinking of the nearby city of

oil refineries and shipping companies near the L.A. Harbor. Good for curses, I'd bet, though you could use it for anything. It's like how some wines go better with some foods, but it'll all get you drunk.

"Beverly Hills," she says, not happy with my assessment.

"Right," I say, putting the cap back. I know Beverly Hills magic. Has the tang of steel, the bite of cocaine, the stink of burning money. But there's no point in antagonizing her.

Alex had a side business selling liquid magic out of his bar. His setup makes these guys look like the amateurs they are. They've only managed to siphon bits from a pool, but he had a thing called an Ebony Cage under the floorboards. Woven basket of living demons' bones, their souls trapped by the magic. Ugly thing, but if you know how to work it you can milk all the power you want off the fucking thing and bottle it up. I don't know what happened to it after he died.

Eventually I come to the stall I'm looking for. Jack MacFee. Wide, straw cowboy hat with a feathered hatband. Skin sunburnt and perpetually red, straggly ginger beard like a lazy shrub that spreads out from under his nose to the top of his prodigious gut. Not fat so much as big boned, surrounded by big meat.

His table is covered with candles for luck and wealth, dogeared Tarot decks on clearance, Chinese coins strung on leather cords, surrounded by the detritus of occult paraphernalia, cheap leavings he sells to the rubes who come by his table for a bit of good luck. He keeps the real stuff in the back.

He looks up at me from his folding chair, mouth a grim line. "Was wondering when you were gonna show up," he says. He's got a voice like a rockslide. "Got a call from the cops this morning. Had to do some tap-dancing. Used up a couple charms I was hanging onto for bigger emergencies."

"You're welcome," I say.

He grunts, pulls himself up from his chair. "Around back," he says, pulling aside a flap in the plastic tarp that makes up his booth. "Don't need to go scaring the straights." I follow him into a room put together with more tarp, red glyphs for privacy and silence crudely spray-painted on each wall, the ceiling, the black pavement floor. If anyone's eavesdropping on him they should just hear static.

He pulls a folding chair from behind a stack of cardboard boxes sagging under their own weight. Falls noisily into it. Grabs a can of Michelob from a Coleman cooler, pops it open, chugs it fast. Doesn't offer me one.

"I assume you pulled that stunt so I'd know?" he says, wiping his beard with the back of his sleeve. "Spread the word?"

"Between that and giving his name to the cops I figured people would hear about Kettleman faster than if I'd tried doing it on my own."

He nods. "Yeah. Well, word's spread. But there's some wondering if maybe you did it."

"If I had, you think I'd be here?"

He shrugs. "Probably not. But if you did, I'd like to know. Bad for business."

"I didn't kill him. He was dead when I got there." I

tell him the story, leaving out hearing Alex's voice. To his credit he just listens. His eyebrows go up a couple of times, but he doesn't interrupt. He pulls another beer when I'm finished, drinks it more slowly than the last.

"Huh," he says.

"That it? Some guy does a *Silence of the Lambs* routine and wears Kettleman like a skin suit and you just say 'huh'?"

"The hell am I supposed to say? 'Gosh, that's a fuckin' tragedy'? Fine. It's a fuckin' tragedy. I'll let people know that if they see him it's not really him. But what—" He stops. Cocks his head. Eyes go narrow like he's focusing laser beams at me. Now he's starting to get it.

"You're wonderin' if I set you up," he says.

"And people say you're slow."

"Oh, fuck you. And fuck you for thinkin' that. That meeting took me weeks to arrange."

"And that would have made an awfully good excuse to get him out in the open for somebody else to take him out."

"Please. I ain't that goddamn smart."

"Horseshit. You're plenty smart. No I didn't think it was you. But I had to ask."

He waves it away. "Yeah, whatever. So, what are you gonna do now? Way you tell it, seems whoever killed Kettleman wanted a piece of you, too."

"Maybe. I'm on the fence there. I'm more wondering about that knife. Seems too specific to just have lying around. And there was more than just the skin. He had

Kettleman's memories. Knew shit only Kettleman would know."

"Obsidian skinnin' knife. Steals a person's form, memories. But leaves a ghost?"

"If you can call it that. Never seen one like it."

He laughs. "I doubt that little detail's gonna help much. You know how many people I've met can do what you do? Three. Two of 'em are already dead. I'll ask around. It's not like obsidian knives are just sitting there on the shelves."

It's surprising to hear him volunteer. MacFee's a money-driven man. The surprise must show on my face, because he gets all sour looking.

"Fuck you, this ain't charity. It's in my best interest this guy gets caught," he says. "People gonna start thinking the way you just did. That I set him up and then where the hell am I gonna be? Selling iPods and shit?"

"Thanks. Appreciate it."

"Yeah, whatever. You got a new phone?" I show him a couple burners I picked up at a nearby stall. Give him the numbers. The way I lose shit it's better to have more than one.

"And that other thing?" I say. He reaches down behind the cooler of beer, hands me a crumpled plastic bag. I open it to find a small bottle of ink sealed with wax and a rolled-up piece of paper tied with a black ribbon.

"Don't open the paper until you're ready to ink it," he says. "There's enough in that bottle for that and whatever you want to touch up."

"Thanks." I pull a thick envelope from my coat

pocket and hand it to him. "You sure this is what you want? I can get you cash just as easily." He opens it and pulls out one of the stacks of prepaid phone card bound together with rubber bands. They're stolen, of course.

"Nah, this is perfect. I sell 'em to dealers trying to clean their money, mark 'em up twenty percent. They launder their cash, I make a profit. Win-win." He frowns. "This is more than we agreed on. A lot more."

"Think of it as an apology for the cops calling you this morning."

"That'll do. You need anything else? Ayahuasca? Lamb's blood? I got a *Santera* in Van Nuys who grows her own chickens if you need a black rooster for anything."

"You running a special on sacrificial animals?"

"That or fried chicken. Your choice."

"Don't have a lot of call for that at the moment, but I'll keep it in mind," I say. MacFee's got a handle on quality ingredients. You need a hand of glory, a dog's head, or iron nails soaked in a murderer's blood, he's a good source.

"You do that. Not much call for grave dust since you left town. Nobody here knows what the fuck to do with the stuff."

"Lucky them."

He cracks open his third beer. I wonder if anybody's tried to walk off with any of his merchandise out front then remember who I'm talking to. If anybody tried to rob him they'd probably find themselves cursed with a sudden case of explosive diarrhea.

"I think I might know somebody who can help you

with this knife thing. You ever hear of the Bruja?" I can hear the capital letter.

"I've known some brujas," I say, "but something tells me this is more of a title."

"Sort of. She's new. New-ish. Been making a stink the last couple years up in Skid Row. Keeps to herself. Doing some community outreach shit or something. Works with normals and everything."

"How's that different from every other hedge witch out there?"

He grins. "Aside from the fact she's making the local Sureños piss their pants? She's got firepower. And a hotel full of vampires and shit, man. Keeps them off the streets, or something. Real do-gooder. I don't really know what her deal is, but she's not somebody to fuck around with."

Something pings in my memory, but I don't quite have it. Have I heard of her? Or am I thinking of someone else? It's right there but I can't quite grab it.

"Sounds like a real Mother Teresa type. Why do you think she might know anything?"

"Rumor is she skinned a Mexican Mafia guy a while back. Left his body on the hood of some shot-caller's car. It's not like skinning is something you see a lot of out here."

Point. "Okay. Watch yourself, though. If it's her—"

"It ain't her," he says. "She's all pragmatic and shit. I know her secretary. Girl's got a head on her. Crazy don't hire talent like that."

"Bit of a stretch, but okay. Still, watch yourself."

"Always do. How about you?"

I pull out my pocket watch. With traffic at this time of day it should take me about an hour or so to get back up to L.A. proper. For an artifact that can twist time, it'd be nice if it could speed up a commute.

I hold up the bottle of ink I bought. "Got an appointment. And then I have to track down a friend."

"You have friends?"

He laughs when I flip him off. I just wish I knew the actual answer to that.

Chapter 4

Green Wizard Tattoos on the Venice Beach boardwalk sits in the back of a medical marijuana dispensary with a glowing, green neon cross out front, above the security guard with the conspicuous baton in his hands. Nobody's toking up inside, but the smell of so much pot in one place makes my eyes water. The place is clean with a Zen retreat vibe, dark wood wall panels, bamboo in planters. I make my way past a whiteboard on the wall showing the store's prices, a glass counter holding pipes, lighters, jars of Grape Ape, Blueberry Kush, Sour Diesel, half a dozen others. An orderly line of people filling their prescriptions goes out the door.

I step through a beaded curtain at the back of the shop and get a face full of patchouli. Whether they're burning the incense to cut down on the pot reek from out front or just to up their Deadhead cred, I can't tell.

The shop's pretty standard. Nothing special. Flash on the walls, stuffed into binders on the counter, buzz of tattoo needles. Guy at the front looks up at me as I walk in, sees my suit and tie. Confusion crawls across his face. "Can I help you?" he says.

"Got an appointment with Stacy."

"I got it, Nick," Stacy says, coming through a beaded curtain leading to the back of the shop. Black, almost six feet tall, hair in dreads, ring in her nose. Stacy's one of the best tattoo artists I've ever met. And the only one in L.A. who knows a damn thing about the kind of tats I need. First ink I got was from her, a hamsa, one of those hands with eyes in the middle for warding off evil, on my left shoulder. It works better than you'd expect, but then that's Stacy's knack. She does with ink what I do with the dead.

"Eric Carter," she says. "Goddamn. You look like hell."

"Next to you I've always looked like hell," I say.

She laughs. "Yeah, that's true. Man, it's been, what, fifteen years now? Never thought I'd hear from you again."

"To be honest, neither did I. Thanks for seeing me on such short notice." Last time I saw her was a week before I left L.A. By that time I had about a dozen tattoos that she'd inked. Nothing big. Small charms and wards, things to help me take a punch, keep cops from looking at me too closely. I didn't know a lot of magic back then. Enough to get into trouble, not enough to get back out again.

"You know I normally have a six-month backlog for my services," she says, "but you're special."

"Like Jerry's kids. You know, your name comes up a

lot back east, actually. I'd hoped to catch you at a show in New Jersey a couple years ago, but I was busy."

"In Secaucus? I remember that show. What were you doing out in Jersey?"

Getting my ass handed to me by a pair of demons who were murdering hobos and prostitutes. I finally got them, but I paid for it. "Work," I say.

She looks at me like she's expecting more but I don't give it to her. "Fair enough. You said on the phone you needed something touched up and a new one?"

"We might want to go in the back to talk about this," I say.

"Oh. Right. Sure, come on." She leads me through another beaded curtain and behind a partition at the back of the room with a tattoo table, a stool and her equipment on a counter.

"I've had some more work done since I saw you last, and I need to get some of them touched up." I hand her the bottle of ink. "Got this today from MacFee down in Torrance. Remember him?"

"God, he's still around?" She uncorks it, takes a whiff and her eyes cross from the smell. "This must have cost you a fortune."

"And anything left when we're done is yours if you want it. It'll keep."

"Deal. Show me what you got."

Her eyes widen when I get my shirt off. She gives a low whistle. "Damn, Illustrated Man, when you said you had some more work done you weren't kidding. What do you need touched up?"

"Anything with a scar through it." I point out a few

spots where I've been cut, burned, stabbed or shot. Then to a circle of ravens on my chest. "And this one. Doesn't need ink so much as a little oomph to recharge it."

"Okay. And the new one?"

I hand her the rolled up paper. She unties the ribbon and looks the design over. It's kind of like a triskelion, but there are tiny fractal patterns in it, spikes and jagged edges that are there on purpose. She studies it, frowns. "I've seen designs like this." She gives me a hard look. "What are you hiding from, Eric Carter?"

"Nothing that'll come after you," I say, hoping I'm right.

"Well, this one's going to cost you. You want this design to work I'm gonna have to pump some serious mojo into it. Ten thousand."

"Done," I say. I figured it would be about that much so I came prepared. I pull an envelope full of hundred-dollar bills out of my coat pocket and hand it to her.

She blinks. "What, no haggling?"

"I live cheap and make a lot of money. There's fifteen in there." This is not the kind of tattoo one fucks around with.

"All right, then. Lie down and we'll get started. I can turn the lights down if it's too bright in here for you."

"Sorry?"

"Sunglasses?"

"Oh, no, I'll keep 'em on. Thanks, though."

"Suit yourself."

Having an ink mage work on you is an experience. They don't direct the spells; that's what the designs are for. Instead they power them, give them life. I can feel the magic burning into the ink as she runs the needle over the designs broken by scars. It's not painful, the needle hurts more, but it's an awareness of the magic as it tries to bind with my own. It's delicate work. Get hamfisted about it and not only does the spell not work, but it can backfire and lash out at the artist. Depending on what the design is supposed to do, that can be deadly.

I've got so many spells inked into my skin by now that I can't remember what half of them do. But when she finishes touching one up there's a slight burn through the design and I can feel the shape of each spell. Three of them ward against bullets, one against knives, one to keep mosquitoes away. The drone of the tattoo needle always makes me sleepy, but my paranoia keeps me awake. Especially when she puts on the new tattoo.

We finish up about three hours later. By the time we're done I'm covered in little bandages from the touch-ups and a couple larger ones over the ravens on my chest and a small patch under my ribcage on my back. The ravens always feel a little weird when I get them touched up. They move around on my chest and for the first few hours they don't settle down. I won't feel them by this time tomorrow.

But the new design is a different story. I can feel its magic already. New tats always take a few days to sink in, their magic settling into my skin, becoming part of me. I'll feel that one for a week, easy. It's only a couple inches wide. The size doesn't matter. The magic stored in it does.

"Do I need to go over the aftercare instructions with you?" she says.

"I think I got it by now, thanks."

"Where'd you get that design, anyway?"

"The new one? Guy MacFee knows. Never met him but I've worked with him before. I trust his work. Usually." If I got what I paid for, and it does what it's supposed to, this design Stacy just put on me should make it a lot harder for Santa Muerte, or anybody, to track me magically. It won't do anything for someone following me who has line of sight, but it should help keep me off cameras. Of course, I won't know if it works until I use it.

I had a series of spells set up once to make it really hard for anyone to find me, but Alex cracked it when he tracked me down to tell me about my sister's death. I'd thought about putting it back in place, but it has downsides, too. Made me hard to find, but also interfered with my own ability to track someone down. Made my life a lot harder than it needed to be sometimes, but I thought it was worth it at the time. Couldn't have been more wrong.

"I know some of what's in that design," she says. "You're hiding from something big and unpleasant. Do I want to know what it is? Is it gonna come looking for me for putting that mark on you?"

"No," I say with as much conviction as I can fake. I don't really know if Santa Muerte is going to be a problem for Stacy or not, but I needed to get this done and she's the only one I know in town who can do it.

"I'm gonna hold you to that," she says.

This tattoo is more selective than the defenses I had

in place before. This is specific to most magical tracking like divinations or location spells with some extra bits that should keep gods like Santa Muerte off my back. Should make me fuzzy on their radar, if not downright invisible. It's not tailor-made for Muerte, but it's open-ended enough that it should include her. 'Should' being the operative word here. She's got hooks into me that I can't even see. This just might be like locking the door after the serial killer's already gotten inside the house.

"Appreciate the help on such short notice," I say, buttoning up my shirt.

"Fifteen thousand dollars buys a lot of goodwill. Now go home, leave those bandages alone for a couple hours and get some Aquaphor on them. They'll heal faster than normal, but the skin's still going to be raw for a couple of days. And for fuck sake don't pick at the scabs."

"Thanks for doing this, Stacy."

"Don't let whatever's chasing you catch you, Carter. I hate to see my work go to waste."

———

The drive across L.A. to Alex's old bar in Koreatown takes me a couple hours. I take the surface streets, since the 10 is jammed as usual. I don't know if the bar's still open, or if Tabitha is even working there, but it's the best lead I've got at the moment.

It takes a little while to find it. I haven't been here in months and I'm looking for a nondescript black store-front with a single door and no signage. When I finally figure out where it is it's no wonder I missed it.

It's still a bar, but it's changed. A lot. Simple black has been replaced with bright pink with blue trim. Got a flashy new sign to go with a flashy new name: Kandy Kitty.

It's hideous. I start looking for a parking spot, spy one on the other side of the street. I split across lanes between a FedEx truck and an F-150 with a bed full of day laborers. If it wasn't for how out of place it was between those two, I might not have seen the white Bentley coming up behind them.

L.A.'s a car town with more luxury vehicles than just about any other city, but even here a Bentley's a rarity. Maybe I'm just hypersensitive to it because of last night. Is this one Kettleman's? If it is what the hell is it doing here? Coincidence? The new tattoo should be blocking any new tracking spells. Or maybe the magic just hasn't had time to set. I can still feel it sinking into my skin.

I'm probably just being paranoid, but paranoia has kept me alive more times than I can count. The Bentley's a couple cars behind me, and I can't see through the tinted windshield. I slow down to give it a chance to catch up to me. If it's the guy from last night I want to know and the only way I can think to do that is to see if he does something to give himself away. Looks like I'll be giving the bar a pass.

I hang a left onto a side street and slow down to see if the Bentley keeps up. It does. That doesn't prove anything, so I head a couple more blocks, make another left and another. Sure enough the Bentley's right there behind me. After a few minutes the driver doesn't even try to pretend he's not following me.

I don't know for sure if it's the guy from last night, but the odds that I'd have a run-in with two different white Bentleys are pretty slim. And if it's the same guy, how'd he find me? I take a few more twists and turns, head east on Normandie then cut up toward Wilshire. What I need to do is get him off my ass, figure out how he tracked me down later. But that might be harder than it sounds. Traffic is heavy. Slow going.

I'm not sure I'm going to be able to shake the Bentley in it when I hear Alex's voice say, "You're not going to lose her in the car."

The Mercedes swerves and I almost take out a guy on a bike before I get the car back under control. This time, instead of some disembodied voice whispering in my ear, Alex is sitting right there in the passenger seat, wearing the same clothes he died in.

"You don't say." My heart hammers in my chest.

"Yep. Too much traffic. No room to maneuver. I'm not telling you anything you don't already know."

"No, you're not. Are you even real?"

"What do you think?"

I don't know what to think. I reach out a hand to touch him and stop just short. He's not pegging any of my ghost radar. What if I touch him and he's solid? What if he's not? I've lived my entire life able to see things no one else can. But I've always been sure that they were there, even if I didn't know what they were. And this is no different.

"I think it doesn't really matter at the moment," I say, turning my attention back to the road. "You said I can't lose 'her.'"

"Did I? Whoops. Should I have said 'spoiler alert' first?"

"So you're not me having a psychotic break."

"You sure? How do you know you didn't catch a view of her in the rearview and your subconscious just suppressed it?"

"And why would it do that?"

"Self-loathing? Guilt? The fuck should I know? It's your subconscious. I think it's guilt. You did put a bullet in my brain, after all. Remember? It looked like this."

His head explodes in a shower of blood and bone leaving a ragged stump. I flinch from the spray, crying out as the inside of the car is painted in red, and this time I do lose control of the car, pop it up onto the curb and almost take out a street sign. Blood drips from the ceiling, covers the windshield in a thick layer of red, coats my face.

A split second later it's all gone. Alex, the blood, the bits of bone and brain. But the taste of his blood in my mouth is still there. Thick, coppery. Shaking, I get the car off the curb, ease it back into traffic, ignore the honking horns around me. Goddammit. I'm not sure which pisses me off more, the possibility that something is fucking with me or that I'm fucking with myself.

The Bentley in my rearview pulls me back to the problem at hand. Whatever the fuck the driver is, Alex was right. I'm not going to lose the car in this traffic. If this were a different city I'd get out of the car and disappear in a crowd on foot. Only L.A.'s not a city of walkers. There aren't any crowds to get lost in.

Or maybe there are.

A flash of a memory that isn't mine hits me and my vision blurs for a second before clearing. The accompanying headache isn't great, but sometimes having these ghost memories can actually be useful.

There's a train station nearby on Wilshire. I've never been there, but some ghost I pulled in when Alex died has. Whoever it was must have been a transplant because I get the accompanying thought that L.A. calling their trains a subway is adorable. Not a lot of people use it, but there might be enough that I can blend into the crowd.

I turn onto Wilshire, head back the way I came. I get a little distance between me and the Bentley, hug the curb, wait until I see the station on my right. Then I engage in the time honored L.A. tradition of the hit-and-run by swerving the Mercedes into the fender of a taxicab. I jump out of the car with a pissed off cab driver yelling at me, bolt for the Wilshire/Normandie station. Behind me I hear the Bentley screech to a stop, the horns of pissed off drivers blaring.

This close and I can see the driver. Alex was right. It's a woman with short, blonde hair glaring at me from behind the wheel. Pale, high cheekbones, too much makeup. I run to the station entrance, waving at her as she gets out of the car in the middle of the street. I push my way down the escalator, pass beneath a mural of a parade that curves around the station entrance, down past the ticket machines. They run on the honor system down here and nobody stops me as I run down to the platform just as a train is pulling into the station.

The crowd should be heavy enough for my purposes. Men and women with briefcases and shopping bags, bikers with backpacks. Mothers with strollers, kids yakking on cell phones. I push my way past them and get into the back of the final car. An announcer tells me the next stop is Wilshire and Vermont and it should only take a few minutes to get there.

I start to congratulate myself on giving the driver the slip, figuring that I can get off at the next stop, steal another car and be on my way, when she steps on at the other end of the train car just as the doors are about to close. The train pulls out of the station with a lurch.

I was hoping I'd get a head start and lose her. Now it looks like my best bet is to keep my distance and take the train all the way to Union where the crowd will be biggest. There are about twenty people in this car. Surveillance cameras, cell phones, maybe even a plainclothes cop or two. She's not going to try anything until we get out of here.

And then she goes out of her way to prove me wrong.

"Eric Carter," she yells, her voice thick with an Eastern European accent. Russian, maybe? Hard to tell with the chatter of people, the sound of the train on the tracks, the automated announcer telling us to watch our bags.

It's clear she's looking at me standing here at the back of the car and everybody's attention snaps between us as they try to figure out what's going on. Crazies on a train are nothing new, and already people are muttering to themselves.

"Got the wrong guy, lady," I say. I look at a skater with a Plan B board and a nylon messenger bag standing next to me. "I have no idea who she is." He edges away from me.

"I'm going to skin you alive," she says and pulls a disturbingly familiar-looking obsidian blade out of her jacket pocket. Now she's really got everyone's attention. Most people are edging out of the way, though a couple are getting out of their seats. A lot of texting and taking pictures. No doubt somebody's taking video of her. She glares at the train passengers, sweat beading on her forehead, eyes wide.

"Stay out of my way and I won't kill you, too," she says to them. Her voice is shaking and I get the distinct impression that she's just bitten off more than she can chew.

"Calm down, ma'am," says the guy nearest her. He edges closer to her, not taking his eyes off the knife. "I'm sure we can work out whatever—" She slashes the knife out at him, though he's too far away for it to hit him. He takes the hint and stops moving.

The next stop comes up really soon, and I've got a full car between me and her. All I really need to do is wait and make sure she doesn't make a move. At this point the cops will grab her the moment she steps off the train. They'll ask me some questions, I'll tell them I don't know who the fuck she is and not have to worry about her for a little while.

She must sense this, because a look of panicked desperation crawls across her face like a swarm of cockroaches.

"You're all in my way," she says quietly, sounding more like she's talking to herself than to any of us. "I don't want to kill you. But you're all in my way."

A big "uh-oh" goes off in my head and I can tell this is about to get very, very messy. I start to draw in power from the local pool just in case I need it. She doesn't seem to notice that I'm drawing in power and I can't feel her doing it. That's one surefire way to tell if a mage is in the area. We can all feel it when somebody pulls power from the pool. Can she even cast?

She digs her free hand into a pocket and pulls out a small slip of crumpled paper, smooths it against her pant leg. She's visibly shaking now. Once she has it straightened out she lets it go. It flutters to the floor.

Paper charms are some of the easiest to make. You can embed all kinds of spells onto paper. Love charms, alarms, wards. I use them all the time with Sharpies and *Hello, My Name Is* stickers to get people to think I'm someone else, think I'm some place I'm not, or not pay attention to me at all.

If you're skilled enough and powerful enough you can pack a paper charm with some pretty serious shit. And with that look of screaming panic on the woman's face, I can't imagine this one's anything good.

Between the fact that she's pulled a preprepared charm and that she hasn't drawn any power from the pool, I at least have an answer to one question. She's not the guy I ran into last night wearing some woman's skin. This might not be her real body, but at least I know I'm dealing with two different people.

I don't give the paper a chance to hit the ground. I can't reach it all the way over here, and I doubt I would want to. Instead I throw out a shield that, hopefully, will protect me from the worst of the nastiness it's about to unleash.

I feel a flare of magic in the train car when the paper hits the floor. The slip flares like flash paper and a sudden inferno of green fire engulfs the car.

The flames explode through the enclosed space, rushing past everyone and everything, though nothing ignites. Instead the lights in the car flicker and die, the windows blow out. Cell phones spark, the train's cameras explode. I feel the force of her spell slam against my shield, pushing me hard against the wall of the car, the spectral flames trying to burn through my defenses. The passengers jerk in their seats, convulse like they're having grand mal seizures, fall limp in their seats, or hit the floor.

I feel every one of their deaths.

The sensation of their collective dying is a punch in the gut, their souls separating from their bodies a hammer blow I wasn't expecting. One or two dead I'll feel like a pinprick in the back of my mind. Easy to ignore. But thirty in one shot leaves me reeling, forces me to my knees. A few cast off ghosts as they die, confused, unfocused. The rest are just gone.

A second later it's all over. The train continues on its way, the sound of its passing over the tracks deafening through the blown-out windows. The only things alive in the car are me and the Russian woman at the other end.

We stand there staring at each other a moment, both of us shocked into silence. "They were in the way," she says, her voice barely audible over the sounds of the train.

"Hell of a rationalization for mass murder," I say. Jesus. My vision goes out of focus and I don't know if it's an aftereffect of some of her spell getting through my defenses or because I've never been around such a massive die-off.

She starts to walk down the aisle toward me, eyes unfocused. "I'm going to throw you out onto the tracks," she says. "And then I'm going to drag you into a dark corner and skin you alive. Take your power, take your memories. Take everything you are." I get the distinct impression that she's not talking to me so much as thinking out loud.

Dizzy and unsteady, I get to my feet. "Yeah, I don't think I'm down with that plan. I don't know who the fuck you are lady, or why you and your boyfriend have such a hard-on for DIY taxidermy, but you really should have done your homework before you decided to screw with me."

Her attention snaps onto me out of whatever sick daydream she was having. She laughs, halfway down the aisle. "Look at you. You can barely stand. What are you going to do?"

"Look up the word necromancer some time."

Used to be a time where this would have taken me days of preparation and thousands of dollars in materials, but after I hooked up with Santa Muerte, whether it's because I have some of her power, or if it just unlocked more of my own, things changed. Now what I'm planning is little more than a thought. It's more complicated than I've tried before. After all, thirty people is a lot, but the principle is the same.

I throw out my magic, latch onto the tiny, lingering bits of life left in all those corpses, and squeeze. Something inside me tears, a cold burning inside my chest I've never felt before, driving me back to the floor. Panic runs through me. Am I having a heart attack, or have I pushed myself too far this time? Maybe I've finally run too much juice through the pipes and this is me burning out.

But the magic doesn't fade and I don't die so I figure I've got at least a couple minutes to finish what I started. I push tendrils of unseen force, threads of pure will wrapping around all of these poor bastards who went from bitter commuters to hunks of meat in the blink of an eye. I reach out through those threads, feel their last thoughts, their final panicked moments care of this crazy bitch.

She walks toward me, picking her way gingerly past the corpses, laughing nervously, as if this all some weird joke and could everybody get up now and not be dead? I can't tell if she's fully realized what she's done. Whether she's freaking out because of me or all of the bodies she's just created. How about we make it both?

The hand of one of the corpses, a slack-jawed, empty-eyed girl slumped back in her seat, reaches out and grabs the hem of her sleeve. The woman jerks back, slashing at the body with the knife. The arm doesn't let go. I don't let it let go.

She pulls away, stepping back into another dead commuter, who wraps her in his arms. She screams and stabs back at it, the blade sinking into dead flesh. I bring another corpse up from the floor like I'm pulling on a marionette's strings. Then another, and another, and another.

She's frantic now. Punching, kicking. She screams, swears at me. Calls me names in three different languages. One arm pinned, the other desperately trying to push the corpses away. The knife is useless. She can barely move it with all that dead meat hanging off her.

So this is what it's like to have an undead army.

"Get them off!" she yells, her voice a high-pitched shriek. "Please." Tears are pouring out of her eyes. If she wasn't totally off the rails before she sure as hell is now. She'll have nightmares for years. Not that I'm going to let her.

The train's coming into the station. Maybe a minute, maybe less. I sure as hell don't want to be here when it does. Being the last survivor in a train full of corpses is a recipe for getting shot at by a trigger-happy LAPD and being asked too many questions I can't answer.

So far I only have the corpses weighing her down, holding her in place. But that's not enough. Not for me and sure as hell not for them. I pull myself to my feet, the pain in my chest spreading. I'm still not convinced this isn't a massive coronary. Though the vertigo is passing, I'm still having trouble standing. I head up the aisle toward her, thinking I should grab that knife, but then I hear the automated announcement saying we're coming in to the next station. Crap.

Instead, I edge toward the door as the train slows, brakes shrieking and throwing up sparks. I have one of the corpses pull the rear doors apart. The wind, already blasting through the blown-out windows, roars through the open door. Time to leave.

Once I'm gone the corpses won't keep moving long. But it'll be long enough. I push out my will with all the fury and anger I can to fill those empty brains.

"Kill her," I say, and jump.

Chapter 5

I hit the ground hard, rolling to absorb some of the shock. I feel the flare of magic as spells in my tattoos take most of the impact. I had them added after getting the crap beaten out of me multiple times. A broken nose leaves a lot to be desired.

Even with all that I take a beating. Jumping from a speeding train's gonna leave a mark no matter what. There's a wrenching in my shoulder, pain flares, eclipsing the burn in my chest. The train recedes in the distance and I half roll, half crawl to something like standing and limp toward the side of the tunnel.

First priority is getting as much distance between me and that moving grave pulling into the station as possible. Get off the tracks, get to safety. I'm not as worried about the mass murderer on the train as I am about getting run down by the next train coming. I don't even want to think about getting picked up by the cops.

I find a safe spot, pull out a paper name tag with the

words *Hello, My Name Is* on it and write "You can't see me" on it in black Sharpie. I concentrate, twist reality around a little, then a little more. I don't want this spell coming undone until I'm well and truly the hell out of here. I slap the name tag on my chest and feel the magic in it take hold. It works different on cameras than it does on people, but it should at least fuzz out my image enough that they can't slap my face on the evening news. Sometimes I think Sharpie magic might be the best magic there is.

I check my phone. It's fried. Soot blackens the area around the buttons, the screen. I try to check the battery compartment and the whole thing falls to pieces in my hands. I slip the pieces into my coat pocket. No reason to give the cops something else to track me by. I have no idea if the other one I bought at the swap meet works, but at least it's not smoking.

"There's a maintenance tunnel nearby," Alex says, appearing at my elbow. He's back to having a head.

I jump, stumbling in the darkness. "Fuck, would you quit that?" I say.

"Didn't know you startled so easily," he says. "Or maybe I did? Have you figured out if I'm a hallucination or not, yet?"

"Jury's still out," I say. "What's this about a maintenance tunnel?"

"Hallway, really," he says. "I wonder, did I see it, or did you see it and just don't remember seeing it?"

"Not sure it really matters right now," I say. "Show me."

A minute later we come to a heavy door plastered

with stickers telling me that unauthorized entry is a felony. How cute. I charm the lock and it pops open onto a staircase heading down. Dim yellow lights barely illuminate the gloom. I close the door behind me and fuse the lock with another charm. I lean against the wall and slump to the floor.

"Any idea where this goes?" I say.

Alex shrugs. "Somewhere that isn't here," he says. "You don't look so good."

"I don't feel so good." My shoulder and chest have gotten into a pissing match over which one hates me more and now my knee's starting to get in on the action.

Now that the main danger is past the adrenaline dump is wearing off, and I'm starting to think about what just happened. She killed everyone on that train. Everyone. Thirty people at least. And the spell she used wasn't one that she cast herself. That paper charm was a one-time curse. A doozy, sure, but if she didn't even try to pull in any magic from the local pool, she probably doesn't know how. Someone else made that thing for her. I'm betting the guy who skinned Kettleman. That sure as hell looked like his knife.

I've seen death that's uglier, messier, almost as many corpses, but I was never there when it happened. If someone dies nearby I'll feel it but it's barely more than a pinprick. But thirty at once that close? Some days this necromancy shit sucks.

I shake the thought off. Death isn't anything new to me. Focus on more immediate problems. I rub at the pain in my chest. I don't know what the hell I did. It had something to do with that spell I cast. I've never animated that many corpses at one time. This isn't burnout, the magic came too easily. So what is it?

"People are gonna be freaking out, soon," Alex says. "Cops finding you wandering around in the tunnels might not be the best move for you."

I'd rather just take a nap, but he's right. I can't stay here. I haul myself back to my feet and head down the stairs. When we finally reach the bottom the hallway stretches out ahead of us into darkness.

"How about that crazy bitch who tried to kill me? Any idea why?"

"You are kind of an asshole," he says.

"I think murdering a train full of bystanders kind of wins her the medal."

I pick my way past old office furniture, mildewed boxes, shrink-wrapped pallets of paper. Takes me a few minutes but then I realize that this passage is being used as storage. And it's pretty far in from where I entered, which means there's another door nearby.

"Yeah," Alex says, "but you're still kind of an asshole."

"If this is about the night in the mansion, you were already dead when I shot you," I say.

"You sure about that?"

I stop, turn toward him, look him up and down. "Yes," I say. "I'm sure. I'm also sure you're not a ghost, I'm pretty sure you're not a nervous breakdown. I'm not entirely sure you're you. So you want to tell me just what the fuck you are?"

"How's your shoulder doing?" he says. "Took a pretty nasty spill out there."

"It's been better."

"Yeah? How about your chest? Hurts a lot, doesn't it?"

That stops me. The pain's fading, but still there. It's a cold, hollow feeling. "What about my chest?"

He smiles at me. "You're right," he says. "I'm not a ghost. You're going to want to make a left at that split in the hall, by the way."

"Don't change the subject," I say.

"Stairs leading out," he says, changing the subject anyway. "They'll get you into an area of the Wilshire and Vermont station. You're not supposed to be there, but that's never stopped you before. Oh, and things are a little hectic there at the moment. You know, with a train full of dead people on it. Nice job with the bodies, by the way. That should keep people guessing for a good long while. What do you think they'll say killed them? Toxic gas? Massive electrical short?"

I bend down to move an office desk out of the way. "I'd chalk it up to terrorist attack," I say. They'll probably close the train down for a few weeks. The conspiracy theorists are going to have a field day.

"Could be. Could be. You know it's really too bad she got away."

"What do you mean?" I turn on him but he's gone. There's no flash of light, no pop in the air. He's just there one second and gone the next.

I spin around to see if he's just fucking with me, extend my senses even though I know he's no ghost. Whatever this guy is I'm pretty sure it's not Alex. Maybe. It just doesn't sound like him. That or death has turned him into a bigger dick than I remember.

It takes me another twenty minutes to get to the end of the tunnel, and when I open the door onto the station it's a zoo. I get caught up in the crush of people being herded out to the street. People are speculating about anthrax, a bomb, sarin gas like in that Tokyo subway. If they knew the real truth, they'd all shit bricks.

For all the panic, people are surprisingly orderly. I can see that they're afraid. Outside is a parking lot's worth of cop cars, fire engines and ambulances. News choppers are starting to fill the sky. Paramedics stand around not sure what to do. Hope they brought a lot of body bags.

I push my way through the crowd, hoping I can get out of there before anybody tries to ask me any questions. The name tag should keep most people out of my way, but if anyone in this crowd has even a little bit of talent they'll spot me. I'm almost through to the edge of the throng when I catch it. A whiff of smoke, the overwhelming scent of roses.

I glance over my shoulder and Santa Muerte is staring at me from inside the crowd, bare skull in a perpetual grin, white wedding dress shimmering in the afternoon sunlight. The crowd breaks in front of her as she sweeps her scythe, totally unaware of her presence. I could run, but what the hell would be the point? The new tattoo starts to burn, so I know it's doing something, but the fact that she's here tells me that it's not doing enough.

I freeze, don't make a sound. She advances, inertia creeping inexorably toward me, and stops a few feet away from me. Facing the wrong direction.

"Señora de las Sombras," I say. She whips around to face me and though her eyes are empty pits I could swear it feels like she's struggling to focus on me. Maybe this tattoo isn't doing so bad after all.

"Husband," she says, her voice flat and neutral. I wince at the word. "You're trying to hide from me."

"Doing a pretty piss poor job of it, apparently."

"Yes. Walk with me. Take my hand. We have things to discuss."

A few people, minor talents probably, glance at me talking to nothing. But in this age of Bluetooth headsets people talking to the air in front of them is nothing new.

"The last time I took your hand I got a little more than I bargained for," I say. "So you'll excuse me if I decline. What do you want?"

"I sensed you were in danger. I came to your aid."

"Kind of on the late side."

"I was . . . delayed. Whatever it is you've done has made it difficult to come to your aid."

"Yeah? What about last night? Didn't think I was in danger then? No, I think you're here because I went off your radar and it freaked you out."

She says nothing and I let the silence drag out. It occurs to me that a staring contest with an eyeless death goddess isn't going to get me anywhere, so I turn my back on her and start to walk away.

"Wait," she says. "Please."

That stops me. Please? From her? I glance over my shoulder. "All right. What do you want?"

"You are in danger. But I don't know from what.

Something interfered with my ability to see you last night. And earlier before I found you here."

That's almost as disturbing as hearing her say "please." "What could do that?" I say.

It's not the new tattoo. Aside from the fact that I didn't have it last night, it's pretty clear that it makes it hard for her to focus on me, but not impossible to track. I run my thumb over the wedding ring on my finger. I knew it was too much to hope for that it would actually hide me from her.

"I don't know. And that's why I am, as you say, 'freaked out.'"

I don't trust her, but I trust whoever's blocking her connection to me even less. If the guy who took out Kettleman and the woman on the train have some way to block my connection to Santa Muerte I need to look into it. Carefully.

"Good to know," I say. "Now, if you'll excuse me."

"Be careful," she says. "You're no good to me dead."

"Noted, Señora." I turn from her and start to push my way through the crowd.

"Some of the dead were mine," she says.

"What?"

"The people on the train who died. Some of them came to me. To Mictlan. They told me what happened. Who was that woman who tried to kill you?"

"I don't know. I—" I look around at the milling crowd. A few are starting to notice me. Here is not the place to start talking about dead people on the train. "I don't know. But I'm going to find out. Thank you for your—" I search for the right word, come up short.

"Concern. Now unless you want me to do something, you can go fuck off." This time I keep pushing through the crowd and I don't look back. The smell of smoke and roses fades a few moments later.

Dammit. I had hoped that the new tattoo would get in the way of her finding me. But it seems something else is doing that for me. Could it be Alex? Could it be something about him that's blocking me from her? For that matter, with the tattoo, how is he able to find me? The spell doesn't include ghosts, but I'm still having trouble believing that he is one.

I get a few blocks away from the station before stealing another car. Today's ride is a gray Honda Accord. Most of the time I prefer cars that are a few years out of date, that don't look too clean. Shabby doesn't grab attention.

Not long back I had a '73 Cadillac Eldorado I got off another necromancer I threw down with in Texas. Steered like a mule, but it was a sweet ride. Two and a half tons of fine American steel. Lost it down in San Pedro when I drove it over to the land of the dead and couldn't bring it back. Long story. I really miss that car.

An hour later I'm back in Burbank, my body in agony. On the plus side I don't have a broken nose and none of my ribs seem to be out of place, and the burning in my chest is gone. I'll take bruises and a sprain to either of those any day.

I strip down and check myself in the mirror. It's always hard to tell where the bruises are amid all my ink, but the worst are easy enough to see. My shoulder is a massive welt of purple and black that spreads down past the scapula.

I wash off in a shower with no water pressure, get the train grime off of me. When I'm done and toweled off I slap a pasty concoction of herbs onto whatever bruises I can reach. Arnica and eucalyptus, mostly, plus some stuff I got from an apothecary in Chinatown, all mixed in with Tiger Balm and a bottle of crushed-up aspirin. Between that and a couple Tylenol I should at least be functional.

I flip on the television to see if there's any more news about the subway. Seems every channel has something. The body count is thirty-two. Lots of speculation, no answers. More importantly no mention of me. I'm okay with that. Hopefully it'll last.

So what do I have so far? One guy wearing Kettleman's skin, a crazy Russian chick with no sense of scale. So far as I can tell they're different people, but when you can take somebody's body by wearing their skin, I suppose anything's possible. Alex's appearance may or may not be a psychotic break. In other words, I have fuck-all.

I lie back onto the bed, exhausted. I start to drift off when my other burner phone lets me know the spell in the train station didn't fry its innards by buzzing on the nightstand. I grab it, half asleep.

"Been calling you the last hour, man. What the hell?" MacFee says when I pick up.

"Other phone got fried," I say. Glad I grabbed the spare.

"I don't know anybody who's as hard on their shit as you, man," he says. "Anyway, she'll talk to you,"

A memory pokes through the fuzz of sleep but I'm not getting it. "Who'll talk to me?"

"The Bruja. She's at some place called the Edgewood Arms in Skid Row." He rattles off an address on San Pedro Street in Downtown L.A. Messy part of town. I make him repeat it twice to make sure I have it. Lots of gentrification, but no matter how many luxury lofts they try to develop or get cops to push the riffraff out, Skid Row is still a mecca for the homeless.

"Wants to see you in an hour."

"Good for her. I'll get there when I get there," I say. Considering how well things went the last time I went on somebody else's timetable, I'm not crazy about repeating the experience.

"I'm just passing on the message," he says. "Do with it what you like."

"I'll check it out. She say anything about the knife when you talked to her?"

"It's more how she said it. She was awful excited on the phone."

"Like, too excited?"

"Maybe."

"Good to know. Thanks." Something's been nagging at the back of my head since I talked to him this morning. "Hey, you said she's got like a vampire army, or something?"

"Fuck, I hope not. No, she just takes care of 'em. They're worse than fuckin' heroin addicts. She owns that hotel, gives them a place to stay. Like some kinda halfway house. I hear she's got other stuff livin' there, too, but I don't know for certain."

"You ever meet her?"

"Nope. Just her secretary. But I've talked to her. Old. Like fuckin' ancient old. That or she smokes fifteen packs a day."

"Thanks. I'll let you know how it goes." I drop the line and start to get dressed. Dammit. What is it about her that I can't remember? Whatever it is I hope it's not important. And if it is, I hope I remember before it's too late.

Chapter 6

The Edgewood is one of those aging single-resident occupancy hotels that sprang up through the first half of the last century in Downtown L.A. The Cecil, Alexandria, King Edward. Icons in their heyday, but gutted husks of former glory, now.

Most have been torn down, redeveloped into office buildings, parking structures, luxury lofts. A few still work as hotels, but that's stretching the definition. Section 8's, drug addicts, people for whom the term "fixed income" means "crushing poverty." They still get the occasional tourist, though some are better known for their serial killer residents. Ever heard the phrase "murder hotel"? This would be the place.

I park the Honda in one of the ubiquitous public lots dotting Downtown just as the sun is setting and take a tour of the neighborhood. The block that the Edgewood Arms is on is surprisingly free of graffiti. Usually you'd see something from the rampant gangs that use Skid Row as an open-air drug market.

But here there's nothing. Streets and storefronts are shabby, but clean, new trees planted, no mini homeless camps of tarp-covered shopping carts shoved into alleyways. The few homeless I do see look like they're either passing through or are actively on their way to do something, not just milling around drinking 40s out of paper bags.

The weirdest thing is the lack of Dead. Skid Row is crawling with them. Homeless who spent one night too many outside in the winter, got shanked for a blanket, or just dropped dead from tuberculosis. Some of them go on their merry way, but a lot of them stick around, little balls of ghostly trauma lingering around the edges.

But this block is empty. Just clearing a house of ghosts is a major undertaking, and to do it for an entire city block and make sure no new ghosts wander in? That's the shit right there.

The Edgewood Arms itself fits the same theme of shabby cleanliness as the rest of the block, like some alcoholic who's come off a bender and gotten a shower and a shave. It needs work, but it's solid. The marble entryway is pockmarked from years of neglect, the portico columns chipped and worn. But the floor has been swept and there's a fresh coat of paint on everything.

I circle the building a couple of times and the charms on the walls are pretty easy to pick out. Don't-look-at-me spells inscribed on the walls tell the normals that there's nothing to see here. Wards against a wide range of demons and monsters and a handful of curses that do god knows what tell the magic types to stay the fuck away. If you're coming in through that front door, you better be loaded for bear.

This isn't a hotel, it's a fucking fortress.

I top off my tank from the local magic pool. I pull in power hard and fast and keep it coming until I can't hold anymore. I don't really need to, but any mages in the area are going to notice and it'll make their ears perk up. The Bruja has shown me hers, the least I can do is show her mine. She ought to know that I'm not someone to fuck with either.

I step through the doors into a carpeted foyer that continues the same, shabby theme. Old carpets, thread-bare chairs, a massive hanging clock with a slowly ticking pendulum. The front desk is barred with an old Mexican guy reading a newspaper behind it. A half dozen Latino men, boys really, barely out of high school, sit in the chairs shooting the shit.

The one person standing out from the rest is a young Latina woman with her hair pulled back in a ponytail sitting in the corner watching me like I'm a snake. Could be that secretary of the Bruja's MacFee mentioned. Probably a mage herself and noticed the big drink I took outside.

And then I see the door and it all clicks.

It's a fancy door. Red leather with brass buttons like you'd see leading to a bar in a Rat Pack movie. Big brass handle, heavy hinges. Only it doesn't go any-where. If this door opened it should open onto the street. Except there's no door on the street side.

That's not the weird part.

The weird part is that along the edges there are letters in Aramaic, script so thin and faded that if you'd never seen the letters before you might not catch them. They're written on doors scattered all over L.A. Some of those doors move. Some stick around for a while. Most don't actually look like doors. I know of one in Catalina, one in a bathroom stall in Union Station.

There are other doors that don't have that script. Doors that open onto places that, believe me, you don't want to go. But these doors open onto a little pocket world stuffed inside a bottle buried somewhere in Los Angeles that's been here ever since a Spanish explorer lost it while he was tromping through the New World. God help us if anybody digs that bottle up.

I make a beeline toward the woman, ignore the stares from the boys and the guy behind the desk. She's young, petite, wearing Doc Martens and a Sleigh Bells t-shirt. Early twenties. Chewing bubblegum.

I've never met her, and I don't know her name, but I've been told about her. At length. Anybody else would look at her and see a clichéd Manic Pixie Dream Girl. Cute, bubbly, maybe a little awkward.

It's all horseshit, of course. She runs this hotel as a home for wayward supernaturals. Vampires, mostly, but who knows what else. From what I've heard she's quite the asskicker. Could tear a hole through this city it could fall through.

Her face changes from wary attention to vapid smile as I get close. Disarming. Good strategy if I were just some no-nothing schlub. I stop in front of her. She looks up at me, blows a big, pink bubble of gum until it pops. The guys in the room stop talking, the testosterone stink coming off of them like they think their baby sister is being threatened.

"They don't even know, do they?" I say so only she can hear it.

"And you're not going to tell them," she says back.

I nod back toward the red leather door. "Darius speaks rather highly of you." Wouldn't shut up about her, in fact. Darius is the Djinn who lives behind that door. When I saw him some months back he was going on about some asskicker witch that had him all hot and bothered. I could be wrong that this is her, I suppose, but I know I'm not.

"Really? He's never mentioned you."

Not surprising. "We're not exactly on speaking terms at the moment," I say. "How's he doing?"

"As pet demons go, he's not bad."

I can't help but laugh, which I'm sure isn't winning me any points. "Is that what he told you he is? Typical." Probably said that to make her feel more in control. Mages know how to deal with demons. We know how to bend our will around them. But I don't know anybody who knows how to handle the Djinn.

"Look," I say, "I don't want to waste your time. You probably don't give a rat's ass about mine. So why don't we go have a quiet chat someplace else without the entourage? Bruja."

She looks past me at the raging testosterone glaring holes in my back and waves them down. "All good,"

she says. "Gonna take him upstairs to meet the Bruja."
She glares at me.

"You sure, you're gonna be okay?" one of them says,
standing up and puffing out his chest. If he's older than
twenty I'd be shocked. Fat around the middle. Trying
to show the others that he knows what it is to be a man.

"He's not gonna try anything, Dante. You know
she's got this whole place hexed." She stands up, heads
toward a cage elevator next to a wide staircase that
used to be grand. I start to follow her and the fat guy
comes up and taps me on the shoulder.

"Don't you fuck with her, *pendejo*," he says. "Or you
answer to me."

I lower my sunglasses so he can get a really good
look at these pitch black eyes. Smile at him. He takes an
involuntary step back, uncertainty on his face.

"Bring it. If you think you're man enough, *chamaquita*."

"Dante," she says. "Your dick's too small to be
swingin' around. Cut it the fuck out." The other boys
all laugh as I join her in the elevator. She closes the gate
and pushes the button for the fourth floor.

I'm not crazy about being in an enclosed space with
another mage I don't know, but considering that she's
already got more composure than the crazy train lady
and more brains than the guy who didn't think of hiding Kettleman's body better, I figure it's a good bet
she's not associated with either of them. Of course, I've
been wrong before.

"What'd you show him?" she asks. "He almost
pissed himself back there."

"My sparkling personality." I take off my sunglasses so she can see. It's just her and me in here and I don't have to worry about scaring the straights.

"Cosmetics by Santa Muerte, huh? I lied a little back there. Darius has told me about you." That might not be a good thing.

"So those kids really don't know you're the Bruja?"

"Please. Would you trust normals to keep a secret like that? They're muscle," she says. "Easier to keep folks off my ass if they think she's some scary old crone. A lot of people don't know I'm the Bruja. So, congratulations, you're in an exclusive club."

"Promise I won't tell," I say. The elevator comes to a rickety stop at a carpeted hallway lined with numbered doors. She pulls the gate open. I step out and move to the side to give her room.

"Oh, I'll make sure of that," she says. I catch the menace in her voice just in time and dodge to the right. It might be the only thing that saves me.

She swings a punch at me, which from a normal would be laughable. But I've yet to meet a mage who doesn't fight dirty. A green haze erupts around her fist and though she only grazes me it feels like I've been sideswiped by a Chevy. The force throws me across the hall and into a door on the opposite wall.

My tats take the brunt of the damage, but I hit the door with my left shoulder and it flares into screaming agony. The door splinters, but holds. Awkward side step as she comes at me. She barely misses. Fist hits the wall. Leaves a spiderweb crater in the plaster.

"The hell is your problem?" I say. Between the

sucker punch and my shoulder screaming I feel like I'm slogging through mud.

"Like you don't fucking know," she says. She spins on me, lashes out with a backhand shot that I barely block with my right forearm. Again, my tats absorb most of the blow. Without them she'd have shattered bone.

"I really don't." With my left shoulder on fire and my right arm going numb from her bone-crunching punch, I opt for a forward kick that I pump with enough juice to send a normal through the wall.

It connects with her chin, a flash of blue light engulfing her as her own defenses take the blow. She staggers back, reeling. Before she can recover, I step forward, send out a right hook that misses by a mile as she ducks in time. She comes up with a fist into my armpit.

Fire explodes in my chest. I double up from the pain. But I'm close enough that she can't get away from me. I hook my foot behind her ankle, slam the heel of my hand into her face and she hits the ground. I pull back to give her a kick.

I don't get very far. She pushes out with her hands and a blast of hurricane-force wind grabs me and throws me clear down the hall. I hit the threadbare carpet and skid, the air knocked from my lungs.

I struggle to get to my feet, pull myself to one elbow, vision blurring. My only saving grace is that she's doing the same thing. The corner of her mouth is bleeding. I can see a goose egg forming on her forehead where I hit her and her face is starting to swell where my foot connected. I crawl to a door, use the knob to pull myself up.

I'm trying to hide the pain, but I know I'm doing a

piss-poor job. Between jumping off a train and getting hammered by magically enhanced punches, I'm not at my best. Having my ass handed to me by a woman a foot shorter and sixty pounds lighter than I am isn't doing anything for my ego, either.

"Come here to finish the job?" she says through gritted teeth. She gets to her feet, wobbles a bit. Neither of us is in much shape to fight. "Thought I wouldn't see through that face?"

"Jesus fuck, lady. Who the hell do you think I—" And then I have an "Aha!" moment. "You think I'm the Russian, don't you? Running around skinning people? Or you think I'm his crazy girlfriend?"

"You think I'm gonna fall for this shit, again? You're out of your fucking mind. Where's the knife, you sonofabitch?"

"I'm not who you think I am. Really." I cough, spit out some blood. Goddamn, she hits hard. "And I don't have the knife."

She bolts down the hall toward me, picking up inhuman speed with every step. I don't have much time, and though we're pretty evenly matched, one of us is going to wind up seriously fucked up if it goes on much longer. I'm more than a little worried it might be me.

I reach into my coat pocket, pull out my straight razor, flip it open. Though I probably don't need blood for this spell I'm already bleeding, so what the hell. I wipe some from my chin, flick it into the air.

One benefit of my particular knack with the dead is being able to see their world overlaid on top of ours. Another benefit is being able to move into it.

I flip over into that purgatory the ghosts hang out in before they fade off to their respective afterlives just as the Bruja reaches me. Physically, I haven't gone anywhere. I'm still in the same place. Fortunately, this is an old building and it's been on the psychic landscape long enough that over here it's just as solid as it is over on the living side. In a new building I might find myself falling through empty air.

Important safety tip: don't try this in an airplane.

The air around me has gone cold and stale, sucking at my lungs, pulling at my energy. This is a world of accelerated entropy. Everything drains fast over here, magic, life, willpower. It's no wonder the ghosts want to consume the living. There's nothing here but emptiness and anguish. Sounds are dull and muted, color nothing but grays and blues.

Though the Bruja's in the land of the living and I'm over here on the dead side, I can feel her passing through me, an icy chill as we step through each other's bodies. To me she's a vaguely human shaped glow, but unless she can see over onto this side, to her I've completely disappeared.

I turn, watch her glowing form stumble as she tries to stop before slamming into the wall. I reach around her with one arm, ready the straight razor with the other. I can't touch her from here. She's as insubstantial to me on this side as a ghost is to me on the other. But that's fine. I'm not planning on staying here.

I pull myself back into the land of the living, sound and color a synesthetic explosion, the Bruja snapping into solidity in front of me. I wrap her in a headlock with my free arm, swing the straight razor at her neck.

And stop just as it dimples her throat. She freezes.

"I can kill you right now," I say. My voice is a ragged wheeze, every breath is like sucking on fire. "But I'm not going to. Because I'm not the guy you think I am and I don't have the knife you think I do. Believe it or not, we're on the same side. I'm betting he tried to kill you because he tried to kill me, too. Now can I put this away and not have you beat the crap out of me? Please?"

She doesn't say anything for a while and I'm beginning to worry that she's prepping some nasty spell in her head. I really don't want to have to kill her. But better her than me. I'm all set to swipe the blade across her throat when she finally says, "Okay."

"Really? No trying to take my head off?"

"You're the one with the razor," she says. I think about that for a second.

"Good point. Let's start over." This is such a bad idea, but if it goes to shit I'm really not any worse off than I was a minute ago. I count to three in my head, let her go. We both push away from each other like jumping away from rattlesnakes.

"Truce?" I say. She turns, anger and exhaustion in her eyes. I fold the razor, slip it back into my coat pocket. Spread my arms wide open. I worry that I've made a really big mistake.

"Truce," she says. Her voice is a lisp from a fat lip, a black and purple bruise spreading across her cheek. I let out a breath I hadn't realized I was holding.

"Thank you." I slump against the wall, slide down to the floor. At this point if she's going to kill me I just might let her.

She slumps to the floor next to me. "Sorry about that," she says. "But I can't afford to fuck around."

I wave it away. "Don't worry about it. I'd have done the same thing."

"Yeah?"

I think about it a second. If I thought the Russian guy was coming for me dressed as somebody else? "Probably just shot you, actually."

"I should try that next time. You want a drink?"

"God, yes."

Chapter 7

"Something I can call you besides Bruja?" I say.

"Gabriela," she says, sliding a couple Advil across the desk at me. "Gabriela Cortez. Take these. Look like you could use them." She pulls a half-empty bottle of Sauza out of a desk drawer and a couple of plastic tumblers. Pours a shot into each.

We've taken the parley to a room converted into an office at the end of the hall. Floral wallpaper peeling in long strips, stink of old cigarettes ground into patchy carpet. Window looking down onto a Skid Row alley, big map of Los Angeles with pins stuck all over it on one wall. She sits in a creaking, wooden desk chair leaning over an oak desk. Digs scattered pills of Advil out of a first aid kit. Cold pack pressed against her cheek that she got out of a minifridge in the corner. The fridge has a little freezer in the top half. In the bottom are row upon row of medical blood bags.

"Thanks." I toss back the pills with the shot. Advil

and tequila. Asskicker's communion. "Lot of blood you got in that fridge."

"Got a lot more in the basement. Darius tell you what I do here?"

"Something about bettering the lives of L.A.'s hidden homeless?" A lot of supernaturals, vampires, shapechangers, shit like that, they don't do so well in the real world, even the ones who look human, or used to be human.

There's never been a lot of them, and they've always gotten a bad rap. Some of it deserved, sure. Nobody's going to say a Wendigo isn't fucking dangerous. But like bears that wander into somebody's backyard, they're usually more freaked out about you than you are about them. So they hide. As well as they can, at least.

She laughs, but there's no humor in it. "One way to put it, I suppose." She points to the map on the wall. "That's the concentration of homeless in L.A. Green pins are human. Red ones means there's at least a couple non-human in the mix."

"Lot of red here."

"That's because of me. Five years ago they were all over the place. I bought the hotel. Got the word out. Have about a dozen living here now. Mostly vamps. A couple other things. A few come in just when they want a shower. Lot more out there. They still don't trust me. I give 'em a home. Keep them off the streets."

"Where they can't hurt anybody?"

She shrugs. "That's a little racist, isn't it? Sure, but that's not why I do it. Vampires are victims. Addicts.

Not just blood, but other stuff. And they hardly ever kill anymore."

"Fair enough." I could tell her a few stories about a group I met in South Dakota a few years ago, but keep it to myself. Out in the country they don't have the kinds of checks on their behavior that you have in a big city. Never really been sure why, though. It can't all be fear of being found out by normals.

She throws back her shot, doesn't even wince. Even with that puffed-out bruise on her cheek, she's girl-next-door pretty. But the way she slams back her tequila and handed my ass to me out in the hallway, it's clear she's a hell of a lot more than that.

"So why do you do it?" I say.

"I doubt you'd understand."

"Why do you say that?"

"You have to ask? Half the mages I run into try to kill me. The rest want a piece of what I've built. Seem to think I'm building an army or something. All they see is power."

"This is your family," I say. "Isn't it? Your community."

"Huh. Maybe you do get it."

"I wouldn't go that far," I say. "It's not something I'd choose."

"It's not for everybody, that's for sure. This is a duty. Nobody else is going to speak for these people. Why not me?"

I think back to a cab driver I killed a few months ago. He'd been murdering young men and women living on the street. Hustlers and prostitutes, mostly. Defenseless people who could barely take care of themselves. I found him when I ran into a ghost of one of his victims in the back of his cab. I bled him on a road in the Santa Monica mountains and fed him to a crowd of hungry ghosts.

"Now that's something I can understand." I sip my tequila. It burns in my throat. "I have some guesses as to why you thought I was the Russian guy," I say, changing the subject. "But I'd rather just hear it from you." I stretch my back and pain flares through my left arm.

"What do you know about the knife?" she says.

"Mostly that two people have tried to kill me with it. Or that there's two knives, I'm not sure. They both tell me they're going to wear my skin like a suit. Seen one of them do it with somebody else's. That's it."

"It's one knife. Best guess is it's a few thousand years old, at least. Legend's kind of fuzzy. Might belong to a god named Xipe Totec, an Aztec farming god who wore the flayed skins of his sacrifices. Maybe somebody else. But it's Aztec."

"A farming god? Who wears dead men's skins?"

"I know, right? The new skin is a metaphor for new growth, crops in fallow ground, that kind of thing."

"The Aztecs were a fucked up people," I say. And this is the pantheon I've married into. I wonder if he's an in-law. Fantastic.

"All the Meso-American gods are pretty much soaking in blood. Hell, it could belong to half a dozen others or none at all, and just had that legend tacked onto it later. No idea."

She sips at her tequila, shifts the ice pack on her bruise a little. "The short of it is that if you skin somebody with it you can take their form, their memories, everything but their actual soul into yourself and call it up whenever you need it."

"Everything but the soul?"

"Yeah. Why, what are you thinking?"

"I ran into the ghost of a guy who was on the receiving end of that knife. It was, I dunno, fragmented. All broken up."

She thinks about it. "Yeah," she says. "Ghosts aren't just souls. They're accumulated experience, thoughts, memories. If he were stripped of everything but his soul that might do it."

I'm surprised and it must show on my face because she laughs. "You're not the only one who knows how to deal with dead people. Neat trick with popping over to the other side, by the way. That is what you did, right? Out in the hall? I wasn't expecting that."

"Yeah. You been there?" The thing with necromancy, or any other knack, is that any mage can learn how to do it. We're all just better at some things than others. I got dead things in spades, but I can't, for example, read auras for shit.

Most mages don't like dealing with the dead except to ask the occasional question or do an exorcism because some Haunt's managed to go poltergeist. And even fewer want to head over to a reality they'll probably see soon enough. So it's a pretty small group.

"Couple times. Kinda fucks me up, though."

"Stay there too long and it'll fuck anybody up. Back to my original question. What about the Russian?"

"I don't know who he is. I think he might have worked for a guy named Ben Griffin who was running rackets around the mage set. I heard somebody took him out a few months ago."

"Awesome. Can't win for losing."

"Sorry?"

"I'm the one who killed him. Sort of."

"So you're the one I get to thank for the power vacuum."

"Brought the cockroaches out?"

"And then some. It's had its ups and downs. Nobody's been able to pull everyone together, but there are a lot of people trying. I think this guy's one of them."

"So you think this is a power grab? He was looking for some heavy artillery?"

She shakes her head. "I thought that at first, but it doesn't scan. How'd he even know about the knife? I had it in a warehouse down in Compton and—"

"Whoa, wait. *You* had the knife?"

"Yeah," she says. "Been in my family a few hundred years. What, you don't think I picked Bruja as a name just because it sounded good, did you? My mother came up from Mexico and tried to get out of the family business. Didn't work out so well. So when I came along and showed signs of magic she carted me down to my grandmother to learn the trade. When I came back I had crates full of random shit we've been guarding for generations. The knife was just part of it."

She pours me another shot of tequila. "But like I was saying, I had the knife in a warehouse in Compton. He broke in with a half-dozen guys last week, killed some of my people. I was lucky I was down there, or he would have killed a lot more. As it is I managed to get his crew, but I missed him."

"So when you heard I was asking around about an obsidian knife and wanted to see you," I say, "you figured he'd skinned me and was trying to sneak in to finish you off?"

"Something like that, yeah. I don't know who the hell I can trust, anymore. If he can take anybody's body, all of their knowledge, how do I even know any of my people are even who they say they are? I tried vetting you when I got your name. Checked with Darius and he told me everything he knew about you. Including your deal with Santa Muerte. She as stone cold a bitch as I've heard?"

"Worse, probably. Darius tell you about my sister?"

"Some, yeah."

"She murdered her to get me back here. Twisted things around so I'd end up tied to her." I show her the ring on my finger.

"Why'd you do it?"

I've been asking myself that question for weeks now. Trying to find some angle where I could have said no. "I was thinking I didn't have any choices left. Did Darius vouch for me?"

"Sort of. But you know him. He's all fucking cryptic and shit. 'If he's him you can trust him, but if he ain't you best give him a wide berth.' Is he really a Djinn?"

"Near as I can tell. Looks like he came to California with the Spanish. And then his bottle disappeared and nobody's found it, yet. It's around here, somewhere."

"What happens if somebody gets hold of it?" She looks thoughtful, and I can't tell if she's thinking of looking for his bottle herself, or if she's reexamining her relationship with Darius. Probably both.

"Don't know," I say. "Nothing good, probably."

"You said you've run into two people," she says. "With the knife."

"Yeah. The guy and some woman. Figure she's Russian, too. Sounds it, at least. With him I thought I might have just been in the wrong place at the wrong time. I was meeting somebody who might have been able to help me get out of this situation with Santa Muerte. But then I caught her tailing me. Things got hairy on the Metro over on Wilshire and—"

"Shit, the train? That was you? It's been on the news all day."

"It was her. Let me be clear on that. Somebody gave her a really nasty spell that took everybody out on that car when they got between us. She's out of her fucking mind."

"Christ. I don't like this," she says. "It was bad enough when I thought it was just a pissy little power grab, but if they're targeting you . . . Oh, this is not good."

"How do you think I feel? I almost ended up this jackhole's skin suit."

"I think this might still be a power grab, but I don't think it's that simple. Aztec blade, Santa Muerte. You."

"That hadn't even occurred to me." Could this guy be trying to get to Santa Muerte through me? Hell, if that were the case all he'd have to do is ask. I'd be happy to put her head on a stick for him if I knew how.

I start to say that but before anything comes out of my mouth there's a presence next to me, a feeling like I'm being watched, which is more than I've been getting so far when he shows up. I turn my head and there's Alex leaning against the map on the wall with all its pushpins and multicolored circles.

"You need to get out of here," he says.

Gabriela sees me staring at the wall. "What is it?"

"You might not believe me, but there's a dead friend of mine standing over there telling us we have to leave."

She looks to the wall, looks to me. Even with other mages I usually get the "He's off his Thorazine" look, but she takes it all in stride. "Okay. Ghost? I've got this place pretty heavily warded against—"

"He's not a ghost. I don't know what he is, but it's not that."

"You called me your friend," Alex says. "I'm touched. That's better than hallucination. But seriously, there's a small army heading here. If you don't get out now, you're not going to get out at all."

"How many?"

"Twenty? Thirty? I dunno. Just a lot, okay? You need to move."

I tell Gabriela this and before I can finish the sentence she reaches under the desk and hits a button. Old alarm bells go off throughout the building, tinny klaxons that sound like grade school fire alarms. She grabs the phone on her desk.

"Trouble. Get people ready." She pauses, listening to the person on the other end of the line. "Unless they can blow open the back door, no, they'll be coming through the front."

I stand up, pain shooting through my side where she threw me into the door. Between that and jumping out of the train I don't even want to think about what the bruises are going to look like tomorrow. I need more information. I go to ask Alex what they're armed with, what their plan is. But he's gone. "Dammit."

"That doesn't sound good." Gabriela says. "More trouble from your friend?"

"Hope not. He's gone."

"He do that a lot?"

"Seems to, yeah."

She reaches behind a filing cabinet and pulls out a machete with a blade more than two feet long. Looks like you could guillotine a fucking elephant with it. Which, I guess, is kind of the point.

"You're awfully prepared," I say.

"Some guys from La Eme used to try this shit all the time. No idea what they were fucking with, but they caught us with our pants down once. That's never happening again."

An emaciated woman peers in through the door. Stringy brown hair, jeans and a purple tank top. Wide eyes, sallow skin, sores at the corners of her mouth.

Arms are pockmarked with needle tracks. I think junkie and then I smell the blood on her. Vampires don't drink the stuff, but you can smell it on them, anyway.

"Jean, get everybody up. We've got a fight coming."

"How long?" she says, hunger greedy in her eyes.

"Not long enough for a hit," Gabriela says. "I'm sorry." The woman's face falls. "Hey, you knew what you were signing up for. You want a place to stay you fucking well fight for it."

Gabriela's tone is a sharp slap. A touch of brutal honesty, but not without compassion. I can see how she's managed to carve this niche out for herself. And how she's managed to keep it. Jean nods and disappears down the hall, banging on doors.

"One of your 'hidden homeless'?"

Gabriela nods. "Sort of the unofficial spokesperson for the rest. She used to be somebody, I guess." She heads to the door. I draw the Browning from the holster at the small of my back, start to follow her out to the hallway. She freezes halfway through the door.

"Fire escape," she yells. I don't even bother looking, just turn and pop off a couple of rounds. Glass shatters, I hear a scream and clanging of metal as whoever I hit rolls down the stairs.

We dive low out of the room. I take up position at the doorjamb, ready to shoot. She ducks behind me. Return fire punches through the plaster walls over our heads. She's got her eyes closed tight, deep in concentration. A moment later they pop open and she swears.

"You all right?"

"I've got wards on every door, window and fire escape for this building. If someone comes near I know it. And they just walked right through them like they didn't exist," she says. "None of my alarms tripped."

More bullets blast through the open doorway. We're going to have to get past it to get to the stairs or the elevator at the end of the hall. Some of Gabriela's emaciated vampires stand at the end of the hallway, unsure what to do. I don't blame them. I'm not entirely sure what to do, either.

"Kettleman," I say. "The guy the Russian skinned the other night was Harvey Kettleman." Every spell has a counterspell and a mage like Kettleman would know his shit well enough to take her wards down. So even if the Russian didn't know how to deal with Gabriela's magic before he sure as hell does now.

"Would have been good to know that before," she says.

"Would it have helped?"

"No, but this gives me something to bitch about besides my own arrogance."

There's a sound of breaking glass from inside the office as someone brushes what's left of it out of the window frame. Shoes crunch as the invaders start to step through.

I shove the Browning through the open door and fire blind. Screams. Bodies hit the floor. I pull my hand back in time to avoid the return volley.

"Any idea if they've come up through other rooms?" I ask.

"Not if they can just waltz through my fucking alarms," she says. "Goddammit. This is going to take me weeks to clean up." She digs into the pocket of her jeans, pulls out a red glass marble.

"Might want to cover your ears." She reaches past me, flicks the marble through the open door with her thumb, turns away with her eyes closed, slams her hands over her ears.

I do the same as well as I can. I've got a gun in my hand and I'm sure as hell not going to drop it. A second later there's a quiet pop and I think, well, that's not so bad.

And then the whole office explodes. Glass and wood, bits of paper and insulation, chunks of bone, muscle, skin all blast through the open doorway, pepper the opposite wall. There's no flame, no heat. Just an immense pressure that pulps everything in the office, blowing out the windows. I start to move and she grabs my hand, hard, yanking me backward.

Good thing, too. The show's not over. The air, full of plaster dust and vaporized blood, pulls back into the office with a sound like a jet engine. Debris sucks back in, pulls the oxygen from the hallway. I can feel the pressure tugging at my clothes, my lungs straining.

An earsplitting shriek, a flash of bright blue and the walls of the office bow in. And then silence. Except for the high pitched ringing in my ears.

"Is it over?" I yell. I can barely hear my own voice. I haven't been this deaf since I saw a Danzig show in the nineties.

"Yes," she yells back.

"Tell me my hearing's coming back."

She pulls pieces of some kind of woody root from

her pocket, hands one to me, pops the other in her mouth. "Chew this. You'll be fine."

It is the nastiest shit I have ever tasted, but I chew it anyway. A few seconds later, my hearing goes back to normal. Some of the pain in my side subsides, too. I'll have to get more of this stuff.

I poke my head through the doorway. The windows are gone. Torn-out holes edged with exposed brick. Carpet stripped from the floor, walls scoured bare. All the furniture is gone. There isn't even a speck of blood.

"You got any more of those?" I ask.

"A couple." She grins. "Want one?"

"Fuck, yes."

She digs another marble out of her pocket, drops it in my hand. "It'll fill the space of whatever you set it off in. A room, a suitcase, doesn't matter." She waves her hand over it and it flashes blue. "It's attuned to you now. Think hard about setting it off and it'll go off. Don't use it in my hotel."

"Deal. And thanks."

Jean and the other vamps run up to us from the end of the hall, pausing at the doorway and gaping in awe at the negative devastation. There's just nothing left in the room.

"I called some of the others," Jean says. "They should already be down—" She's interrupted by screams and gunfire coming from the lobby. Gabriela bolts for the stairs and the rest of us follow. Two mages, five vampires and whatever she's got downstairs.

The stairs allow for two of us to head down side-by-side. We pause at the second floor landing and duck. A cacophony of gunfire, yelling, screams. I pop my head up and look over the side of the railing.

It's the weirdest bar brawl I've ever seen. Thugs with close-cropped hair, tight leather jackets, button-down shirts going toe-to-toe with a crowd of pissed-off tweakers. The guns aren't as big an advantage against the vampires as these guys seem to think. Sure, a bullet will slow them down, but it won't kill them. It'll do a bang-up job of pissing them off, though.

I see one of them put a couple rounds into a vamp's chest, thick black ooze spreading into his shirt where the bullets punched through. It doesn't even slow him down. He gets the guy into a bear hug, his spindly arms wrapping around him like a spider. But the gangster's gun is between them and he unloads the rest of it into the vamp, dropping him.

Similar scenes are playing out all throughout the lobby. There's at least thirty people down there. A lot of the gangsters are cluing into the fact that putting holes in vampires is a fool's errand, dropping their guns and opting for collapsible batons, instead.

"How is it?" Gabriela says as I duck back.

"Messy," I say. A stray bullet ricochets up through the gap between the stairs and gouges a hole in the wall. "You sure you want to get into that?"

She hefts the machete in her hand. "Nobody comes into my home and shits on my carpet."

She digs into her pocket, pulls out a scrap of paper, wads it into a tight ball, then tosses it over the side of the railing. There's the tiniest of flashes. The gunfire stops. I can hear the click of hammers and triggers, but no rounds fired.

"Did that just turn this into dead weight?" I say, showing her the Browning.

She winces. "Sorry. It'll work again once you get out of the hotel." Great. Using the gun in that mess probably wouldn't be a great move, anyway, and using the pocket watch would be the mother of bad ideas. I pull my straight razor out of my coat pocket, flick it open. I'm going to have to sterilize this thing before I use it on myself again. It's a wonder I don't have Hep C.

Gabriela hefts the machete in her hand, bolts down the stairs. Lets loose a warrior princess shriek like a tiny, pissed off Xena. She's five feet of screaming fury swinging a machete. I don't know if that's badass or suicidal.

All right, then. Let's do this.

We're outnumbered. Three to one, at least. Floor littered with bodies. Mostly Gabriela's men, a few the Russian's. A couple of the vampires are on the floor, slowly leaking out black, oozing blood, massive bullet holes through their skulls, or their chests. That'll slow them down a day or two.

I get to the bottom of the stairs and see two guys on Jean, hitting her with batons. She's not a great fighter, but what she doesn't have in skill she makes up for in not going down. It's not entirely clear she can feel the blows.

I hit the closest from behind. Pull his neck back. Slice the razor deep through his throat. I knee him in the back as his eyes bug out. He stumbles, falls into his buddy. Jean grabs the opportunity, gives a vicious uppercut with an open hand, fingers splayed. Her nails are like spikes, punching up though his jaw. She pulls back, wiry muscles straining. Crack, twist, pull. The man's head comes off his shoulders and she flings it aside like it's a rotten fruit.

Every time I see a vampire fight I wonder how they haven't managed to take over, and then I remember that they have notoriously bad judgment. Sure, they're frighteningly strong, but they've got the addict's mindset, a mess of neuroses. Driven by their addictions, they're barely functional. Thank god for small favors.

I turn to see Gabriela going mano-a-mano with some mobster with a Bowie knife. Another coming up behind her. There are too many people fighting between me and her and a straight razor's not exactly a throwing weapon.

There are a lot of corpses, and plenty of them are leaving ghosts, so I'll have to make this fast. I break into a run toward her, three guys stepping into my path. Before I get to them I flip over to the dead side and pass right through them.

The new ghosts, some of the Russian's men, some of Gabriela's normals, see me immediately. Confused, frightened, too new to know what the hell is going on, they act on whatever passes for instinct in the newly dead and come right at me.

I sidestep one as it takes a swipe at me, get up between Gabriela and the guy coming up behind her and pop back into the real world. I sweep the razor in an S pattern, catch him across the eyes, widen his mouth and finish him off with a deep cut through his throat.

The distraction of my appearance surprises the guy with the Bowie knife and he misses Gabriela's machete swing. Whatever she's magicked that blade with is pretty fucking impressive. It cleaves clean through his arm. She brings the machete back around and chops through his leg, dropping him to the floor. She could finish him off, but instead she nods at me as she moves onto the next guy, leaving him to bleed out.

I immediately get into it with another of the Russian's men, stepping in close to keep his baton from caving my skull in. I take a hit on my already bruised side, the magic in my tattoos flaring to spread out the impact. I catch him on the inside of the wrist with the razor as he brings his baton in for a second hit, but he doesn't drop it.

That's okay. I didn't really expect him to. The important thing is that he's bleeding. I shove my way closer, grab him in a bear hug that takes him to the floor and pop both of us over to the dead side.

The ghosts are on us in a flash. The blood from the razor cut is like chumming the water for sharks. One of them swipes at me, catching me along the back with a hand that bites like ice on fire before I can roll off the mobster and pop back into the real world. I leave him behind for his dead friends to snack on.

I've been hit by ghosts before. It's not fun and my body's not reacting to it well. My back seizes up momentarily, the wound a cauterized furrow in my flesh. It takes me too long to get up.

"Stay down," Gabriela yells. I look up to see a guy

with a hatchet coming at me. She's a good twenty feet away but she throws the machete overhand, anyway. It sails end over end through the air and bites a good three inches into his skull. She gestures for it, and the blade pops out of his head like a cork to fly back into her hand. She has the coolest toys.

I pull myself up from the floor, take a look around. Now that things have gone hand-to-hand, the tide's starting to turn. Gabriela runs through the fight like a mad dervish. Taking advantage of her height, ducking in low to hack through kneecaps. Once a man's on the ground it's pretty much over.

And then I see them. The Russian wearing Kettleman's old man skin suit and the crazy chick from the train walk through the front door. Up close and in the light I still can't tell it's not him. If anything he looks more like Kettleman than he did on the roof of the observatory. Whatever magic is in that obsidian blade has got to be pretty fucking powerful.

The woman, though, she's not looking so hot. Bruised, beat to hell. There's a large, red welt down one side of her face less than an inch from her eye. She has a bandage wrapped around her left hand. I can see blood seeping through it. There are bite marks on her neck. Those dead train passengers really did a number on her. I wonder how she got away.

She sees me from across the room, tugs on the Russian's sleeve and points. He sees me, sees the way the fight is going. I feel him pull power from the local pool. A lot of it. Gabriela pops her head up, blood spattered across her face, matted in her hair. She feels it too.

I'm moving too slow and I'm running low on power. Even if I wanted to cut across the room on the dead side— suicidal at this point, there are more dead in this room than living—I don't have enough juice to do it. I consider just wildly throwing shit in his direction, but before I can do anything he touches the floor with his hand and a wave of power blows out in a ring around him. I've done enough summoning to know he's just called in the cavalry. A flare goes off near the staircase, one by the front desk. I feel displaced air behind me, spin around.

The thing standing there is about seven feet tall, built like a wrestler. Muscles on muscles. Slick, black skin like polished ebony, thin veins of glowing red just under the skin. Where its head should be is a roiling mass of tentacles, whipping around like snakes on fire. Each arm ends in a hand with an open mouth in the palm, needle teeth dripping green goop.

Demons are easy to summon. Seems like they're sitting there in whatever Hell they're hanging out in just waiting for somebody to call their number. All those rituals and chants and circles and candles? That shit's not for them. It's for us. It's the protection that takes a long time. The actual summoning is a snap.

Which means that whatever he's summoned is about as feral as you can get.

The thing throws one of its arms out in a quick jab, latching onto my left shoulder. I bring the straight razor up and slice through the wrist. There's no bone. The blade goes clean through. The thing jerks its arm back and I tear the hand from my shoulder, the teeth ripping out flesh like a lamprey.

The pain fucks my concentration. It's a burning lance of agony. I stagger back, a wave of dizziness washing over me. The thing whips its other arm at me in a haymaker and before I can raise my arm to block it, it punches me in the head. I go crashing into the crowd, landing on the body of one of the Russian's men.

My vision blurs. The left side of my body goes numb. I try to move but paralysis hits me like a freight train. Of course the fucking thing would be venomous. My joints freeze up. Hopefully it isn't so poisonous that it stops my heart. The world around me slows down, fades in and out, goes black.

A second, a minute. I can't tell. When my vision returns the hotel is full of smoke, fire, screaming. Flames are crawling up the walls, spreading across the ceiling. I try to get up, but no dice. The best I can do is roll over to my side and even that's a struggle. Not an improved vantage point. From this angle I can really see how fucked things are.

The fire's an inferno. I see Darius' door engulfed in flames. He'll be fine, but nobody's getting in or out of that door. Bodies burn in the hotel's wreckage. Support beams in the ceiling threaten to collapse. If the poison doesn't kill me I'll be burned to death.

Somebody starts dragging me across the floor. My shoulder is a ragged mess, blood spreading from the wound. I swim in and out of awareness, my vision a series of snapshots as the ceiling crawls past my vision. One second I know where I am, the next I don't.

"If you die it's gonna be really goddamn inconvenient," Gabriela says, pulling me out through the doors. She sounds very far away. I try to say something, but I can barely move my lips, much less make any sound. I think I'm losing a lot of blood.

Then cursing, gunfire. The shattering of glass. Sirens in the distance. I see someone smack Gabriela aside like she's a ragdoll. A man's face blurs in front of my eyes as consciousness fades.

"He won't die yet, *chica*," he says. "We gotta skin him first."

Chapter 8

An empty highway at noon. Mountains in the distance like a moonscape, the land blasted and bare. Skeletal palm trees speed past, dead husks with dried fronds. Air so desiccated the wind blowing in through the Cadillac's window feels like sandpaper.

"This isn't right," I say.

"You're tellin' me," Alex says. He's in the driver's seat, a bottle of beer held between his legs. "This thing steers like a fucking cow."

This is my Eldorado. Well, the Eldorado I stole off a dead mage in Texas. Only I left it in San Pedro when I took the whole car over to the dead side and didn't have enough power to bring it back. Far as I know it's still there.

"No," I say. "You, the car." I wave at the landscape speeding by, surprised I can lift my arm after the beating I took in the hotel. "All this. Where the hell are we, anyway?"

"Nowhere, really. Look, we don't have a lot of time. Well, you don't have a lot of time. I got the stuff comin' out my ass."

"What the hell are you talking about?" There's something familiar about the landscape, about the dryness in the air, the sense of blasted emptiness.

"You're pretty jacked up," he says. "They think they've got your hands tied, and they do. Literally, come to think of it. But you've got an ace. You just need to figure out how to use it."

"This is all going on in my head, isn't it?"

"Mostly. I don't want to be telling you this because it's just going to speed up the inevitable. But you dead isn't going to do either of us any good. Not yet, at least." He takes a pull on his beer.

"You could just tell me what I need to know."

He shakes his head. "I don't even want to be telling you this much. You'll either figure it out, or you won't. And to be honest, I kinda hope you don't."

"Who are you really?"

The car hits a pothole. "Crap," he says. The landscape shudders, the mountains shimmering, fading out, popping back into view. "Okay, this next bit's really gonna suck. Just remember that there's another way out. You just need to grab it."

The Eldorado hits the mother of all potholes, blows out a tire, goes into a skid. I'm thrown against the dashboard, my head snapping forward into the windshield with a loud crack. Everything goes black.

———

I wake to the smell of blood and smoke, the buzz of fluorescent lights. Storage room of some kind, cardboard boxes of no-name big-screens, DVDs, stereos. Some still on pallets wrapped in plastic, others piled high along one wall.

Red, hand-painted scrawls cover the walls. Insane squiggles. Sharp, spastic lines. I recognize some of them. Runes for binding, barriers. I have a few of those inked on my skin. Others I've never seen before. But I get the gist. And it's not good.

Takes me a minute to realize it's not all painted in my blood. Some of it, sure. I sure look like I've bled enough. But it's the guy lying on the floor in front of me with his abdomen torn open and organs pulled out that's the big giveaway.

The demon's venom seems to have worn off. I can move, so that's a plus. I roll myself up to sitting, the pain in my shoulder a burning agony that flares through my chest, and cough soot out of my lungs. My arms being zip-tied behind me aren't helping. Blood, sticky and crusted, has soaked through my shirt. Those little needle teeth sure did a number on me.

I take a closer look at the runes on the wall, looking to see if I'm wrong. A few seconds of parsing out meaning and I know I'm not. All those markings working together have turned this room into a kind of magical Faraday cage. It'd be one thing if it just blocked me from the local pool. I don't need to grab any extra power to pop off some zip-ties and walk out of a room.

But some of the spells in those runes are nullifying, sending out a steady stream of magical static that'll block any spells the way noise-cancelling headphones cut out that screaming baby in the airplane seat next to you. In other words, right now, I'm just as normal as anybody else.

The room doesn't have any windows, and only one flimsy-looking door. I can hear sirens not far off, helicopters overhead. Either that's a different four-alarm fire or I'm holed up in some poor bastard's electronics store downtown.

No magic. No gun. Christ only knows where my razor is. Even if I could get to the pocket watch the only thing I could do with it is tell time. Not real useful in a case like this.

Realistically, all I have to do is get through that door. Unless whoever painted this room with Mr. Proprietor's guts have done the rest of the place up like a Pollock painting.

Takes a bit of doing, but I get to standing. Dizzy from blood loss. First order of business is the zip-tie. There's a trick to getting out. I lean forward at the waist, stretch my arms up and behind me as far as the pain in my torn-up shoulder will let me, then bring them down hard against my tailbone while pulling my hands apart. It's not enough. My shoulder's still more dead weight than not and I can't get enough momentum to break out. I start looking for something sharp to maybe saw through the tie, but there's not so much as a box cutter in here.

The door opens to a redheaded man, freckles scattered across his face, wearing a green suit and tie. Perfectly normal looking except for the glowing red eyes smoldering like coals.

"It's awake," he says, stepping inside. A girl follows him. Looks maybe ten, twelve years old, Shirley Temple curls, Hello Kitty dress. Her eyes aren't glowing red embers, but the irises are an unnatural blue.

"Where's your buddy?" I say. The Lovecraftian horror that bit me in the shoulder is nowhere to be found.

"Your friend killed him," the girl says. "Millennia old and she wiped him out of existence." She flounces into the room, plants herself on a stack of boxes, pouts with her arms crossed. She brightens up. "I helped."

Of course she did. They're demons. That's what they do. Impulsive, psychotic, stupid, but you can always trust them to turn on each other. Pretty low on the supernatural totem pole. Who knows what hell they crawled out of. Doesn't really matter. There are a lot to choose from, after all.

"Can we kill it?" the redhead says. This is the guy who said something about skinning me back at the hotel. I don't see the knife, so I'm betting they're just here to hold me until the Russian shows up with it. At least I hope so. He steps a little closer than I'm comfortable with, but I stand my ground. Sure, he can tear my head off, but I won't give him the satisfaction of flinching.

The girl sighs. Loud, dramatic. You'd almost think she was a real twelve-year-old girl. "No," she says. "Stupid rules."

"Rules, huh? You don't say." My instincts are to keep them talking. Even if they've been given specific commands not to kill me it doesn't mean they'll always listen to them. I try to feel for any chink in the cage keeping the magic out. If I could find a crack I might be able to wedge it open further. I don't need much. Banishing spells are stupid simple. They're some of the first things a mage will learn. The ones who usually don't survive very long.

"I know what you're doing," the girl sings. "But it won't work." She hops off the stack of boxes, spins in place with her arms outstretched, feet dancing in the blood of the corpse at her feet. "That's Nice Mister Iglesias. When we came here he said, 'No, no, no! You must get out!' so I gutted him and shit in his chest then smeared him aaaaallll around the room!"

"Well, aren't you just the cutest thing," I say.

"I am! I looked just like this when I killed a policeman, and a preschool teacher and an old lady who lives with lots of cats. I got them all alone, and I ate 'em up!" She snaps her jaws and her lower mandible unhinges, teeth like swords springing out. She bites the air, retracts her teeth and a second later she's a giggling, innocent little girl again.

I need to get the fuck out of this room.

"So you won't find any holes, Mister Necromancer," she says. "No, sir. The dead won't answer your calls. No one here to help you."

We'll see about that. "So how come you can't kill me? Big, nasty demons like yourselves. Don't tell me somebody's got you on a short leash."

"We answer to no one," the redhead says. He gets in my face and I can smell blood on his breath.

"Horseshit. You answer to the man who brought you here. Must have thought it was your lucky day getting summoned with no protections, no wards.

Then, what, he yanked you back when he needed you? Slapped a collar round your neck and made you beg like a dog? Is that how it worked?" His eyes glow brighter, he punches me in the face with a fist like a sledgehammer.

"He's right and you know it," she says to him. "You're just as owned as I am." She points to me. "And now he owns you, too. He's trying to get you mad. Thinks he can make you do something stupid. And he can, too. Because you are stupid."

I push past the pain, keep poking at the cage with my mind, trying to find something I can worm my way through, but it's as tight as a nun's asshole. There's got to be something. I'll never make it through the door before these two are on me. And I have no doubts that if push comes to shove they'll gut me like they did Nice Mister Iglesias.

What was it Alex said? I've got an ace, I just need to figure out how to use it.

I stop looking outward. Being cut off from the magic is like having a noise you'd spent your whole life with suddenly gone. Things you hadn't heard before, like your own heartbeat, are thundering in your ears. And somewhere, just below my perception is something I'd never noticed before.

It's not magic. Not the way I know it, at least. A small nugget of power rooted deep inside me. Black and seething. Stinks of death, but different. So old it's alien. I think it must be something Santa Muerte gave me, but if she did it doesn't belong to her. I couldn't say how I know, but I know. It feels masculine somehow, and I think that she would probably find it as alien as I do.

"I am not stupid," the redhead says, seething. He spins on the girl, stalks toward her.

The more I examine this little chunk of power, the more it grows in my awareness. It's more than just death. Not like how I've ever understood it. It's not a tool, not a thing I can use. It's not like the power I have to talk to ghosts, or move corpses with my mind, or flip to the other side. Those are things I do. This is the thing itself.

It's not death. It's Death.

"You're very stupid," the girl says. "And you don't deserve what's promised you. All we have to do is keep him here until the man with the knife comes back to skin him and then we get all the souls we can eat. But you're just going to fuck it all up, like you fuck up everything."

The demons are frightening, but this power is downright terrifying. It's a parasite. If I let it, it would consume me whole. At first I think I can feel it spreading through me, but then I realize it's already there. Just sitting, dormant, wrapped up inside me like a coiled snake waiting for me to do something with it. Waiting for me to accept it and let it rule me.

Like it or not, it's my ace.

"He can skin a corpse," the redhead says. "It's just meat, anyway."

"Biggest score in over two hundred years and you want to piss it away because somebody bruised your ego," the girl says. She heaves another one of her theatrical sighs. "I guess I'm just going to have to kill you and take it all for myself."

"I got a better idea," I say, reaching toward that dark power, letting it flow through me to do what it wants. "How about I kill you both?" The zip-tie binding my wrists together disintegrates as the redhead turns to me, lashes out with his hand. A few inches from my head and it vaporizes, breaking into dust that scatters in the air. He screams, his face twisting out of its human shape. His jaw unhinges, three barbed tongues lash out toward me only to meet the same fate. He reels back, his remaining hand pressed tight against his mouth. Smoke boils up from beneath it.

The redhead is closer, so I focus on him. I grab him, his skin blistering and flaking away into dust. I focus my will into this nightmare energy and pump him full of it. He tries to pull away, but it's too late. He stumbles, falls. Pieces of him disintegrate like a sand castle in a high wind. By the time he hits the ground he's nothing but a pile of grit.

"Oh, mister necromancer," the girl says, "you are so very, very interesting. I'm going to have fun playing with you."

I turn to her, intending to destroy her the same way, but then there's a tugging in my chest, a tearing. A burst of pain blows through me. It's the same as on the train, only ten times worse. Through the haze of pain I get it. I didn't push myself on the train when I animated all those corpses, I tapped into this power without realizing it.

The pain is intense and I fight to keep it from dropping me. The girl picks up a box from the stack against the wall with one hand, one of the big-screen TVs, and lobs it at me like it's a baseball. It hits me in the chest, a good fifty pounds of plastic, glass and cardboard, knocking me against the wall. My concentration's blown and the tenuous grasp I had on that power disappears.

She's on me in a flash. Tiny hands stretch, skin splitting until the fingers are sharp, birdlike talons wrapped in shredded flesh. She gets hold of my throat before I can stop her, sinks her claws into my neck.

I struggle, try to push her off me, but it's like she's made out of concrete. I change tactics, root around my psyche for that power. I can feel blood trickling down my neck, soaking into my collar. She's laughing, toying with me. She could just pop my head off here and now. Maybe she's still thinking of that payday the Russian promised her and doesn't want to kill me just yet.

That little bit of hesitation is all I need. I find the thread of that power and pull it like a ripcord. I feel it bloom within me and I throw it out. No direction, no focus. Just let it go where it wants to.

She screams as it takes hold of her, her skin blistering and flaking, disintegrating into dust. Her hands are husks blowing away on a wind that isn't there. She unhinges her jaw to snap at me, one final desperate move to take me out, but when her teeth spring out they flake away before they can touch me. I push her body off of me. My hands sinking into her disintegrating body like it's sand. She's gone in the blink of an eye.

I fall to all fours, gasping for air. The pain has lessened somewhat. Now it's just feels like I've been hit in the chest with a 2x4 instead of a freight train.

With the adrenaline wearing off I'm really feeling the fatigue and the blood loss, not to mention the bruising, cuts, and whatever the fuck she did to my neck. I try to stand, but my vision blurs and dizziness washes over me.

Goddammit. I really need to do something about all this passing out.

Chapter 9

I wake up to someone yelling. I jerk my head up, which turns out to be a bad idea. The room spins like a Tilt-A-Whirl and I almost throw up.

It takes me a second to remember where I am and what's happened. I take stock. Beat to hell, covered in blood, my shoulder a ragged mess of torn flesh. In a room with the gutted corpse of a stranger where the walls have been painted in his own intestines.

"Eric? Holy shit, it is you." An Asian woman kneels down next to me but she's going in and out of focus. It takes me a second to figure out who it is.

"Tabitha?" I look up at her and she recoils. Man, I must look worse than I thought. "Hey. I've been looking for you." I always thought she was cute, but right now she looks like an angel.

I think I might be delirious.

"Eric . . . Jesus. What happened to—Ya know, save

it. We need to get you out of here. You look like a horror show. Can you walk?"

"I have no idea. Let's find out together. Help me up. Or are you a hallucination?"

"I wish," she says. She wedges herself beneath me and pulls me up until I can get my feet under me. I'm wobbly, but I can stand. More or less. "Come on. I'm parked in the alley." She gets under my arm, the good one, thank god. The left is hanging dead at my side. She's not tall, but she's all compact muscle and she's able to support me easily.

I can't feel the power I'd tapped into earlier. Gone dormant, I suppose. I seriously doubt it's gone. It felt as much a part of me as my limbs do.

And that scares the piss out of me.

The flood of magic returns once we get out of the room past the runes. It's like that feeling when your ears pop and you can hear again. Tabitha must feel it too, because she immediately gets more relaxed once we're past the threshold. I wonder if she even knows why.

She helps me through the store. The front is closed with a roll-up gate covering the entrance. Cheap electronics cover every surface. Flat-panel displays on the walls. I don't see any sign of my straight razor, but I do find the Browning sitting on a countertop display of cell phones.

"Hang on," I say. I grab the gun and slide it back into its holster. "Want a new phone?" She shakes her head, confused, as I grab three Nokia knockoffs and stuff them in my pocket. Can't hurt to have a few more. I remember a time I did everything through a messaging service and payphones. I don't know how the hell I managed.

"How'd you find me?" I ask.

She chews the inside of her lip, says nothing for a while, then, "Alex. Jesus, Eric, I saw Alex."

I stop dead. "You saw him?"

"About an hour ago. He just popped up out of nowhere, yelled an address at me and told me I had to get here to save you. Then he disappeared again. Maybe ten seconds all told. I thought I was going crazy."

"You're not crazy," I say. And apparently neither am I. "Wait, an hour ago?" When the hell did she leave home?

"I saw a fucking ghost, Eric. To normal people, that's kind of a big deal. I freaked out a little, okay?" She gets me outside and helps me over to her Mini Cooper parked in the alley outside. I can stand a little better now, but I still need to hold on to the car to keep from falling over.

"I get it," I say. Of course that would happen. Ghosts do that to most people. Talents, normal, doesn't matter. Nobody likes ghosts. She opens the door, helps ease me into the passenger seat. "Thanks for coming to get me."

"I almost didn't," she says. "I thought I was hallucinating."

"Lot of that going around." So Alex appearing isn't me having an episode. If she's seeing him, too, he's not just inside my head. Good to know. I still don't know what the fuck he is, but now I know something he's not.

She pulls out of the alley. We're still in Downtown. When the demons snagged me they didn't take me far. Gabriela's hotel is only a couple blocks away. The air smells of smoke and I can see the blue and red of police and fire truck lights flashing across the street.

I hope she made it out of there.

"We need to get you to a hospital."

"Not a hospital."

I wonder if the spell I put on in the subway tunnel actually worked against the cameras or if my face is plastered all over Los Angeles by now. Getting out of police custody is stupid simple, but I'm not really in the mood for it. Besides, being stuck in a cell or a guarded hospital room, even for a little while, would make it too easy for the Russian to get to me.

"Eric, you're really fucked up. And your eyes—"

Ah, yes. The eyes. "Can we not talk about that just yet?" I test my shoulder. It's moving better than it did when I was tied up and the pain is a lot less. The wound has stopped bleeding, so that's something. Pretty sure the demon's poison has run its course. Still dizzy, but that might be blood loss and exhaustion. I won't know until I look at the wound if it's infected, though. On the plus side, demons don't usually have bacteria that can infect humans, so chances are I'm fine there.

"Fine. Let's not talk about the eyes. But the rest of you is a mess. You need a hospital."

"Trust me. Hospital's not a good idea. Besides, it looks worse than it is."

"Where then? What do you usually do when you get this fucked up?"

"I don't usually get this fucked up. Look, just drop me off at a drugstore and I'll grab some bandages. I'll be fine."

She shoves her hand in my face. "How many fingers am I holding up?"

"Three," I say.

"Two, I'm taking you to the hospital."

"Tabitha, if you take me to the hospital, they'll try to take me to jail. And people might get hurt. People who won't be me."

She tightens her fingers on the steering wheel. Whether working hard not to be freaked out or pissed off, I can't tell. "Fine," she says. She pulls her phone out of her purse.

"Who are you calling?"

"Vivian," she says. "She's a doctor." I grab the phone out of her hand. "What the fuck, Eric?"

"No. Fuck no. You really think she wants to see me? You really think she's going to help me?"

She opens her mouth to say something, but stops. "Okay. Yes. But once I tell her about Alex—"

"She'll freak the fuck out. You want to do that to her? You want to bring him up?"

"But he's back."

"Back is not back. Tabitha, he's dead. Even if he's a ghost, and I'm not sure he is, hell, I'm not sure what you saw was really him, he's still dead. How do you think she's going to take that news?"

She clenches her teeth, tightens her hands on the wheel. "Okay," she says. "No Vivian. So where then?"

"Just drop me off wherever. I can grab a ride."

She laughs. "You have no idea how bad you look, do you?" She pulls onto the 110 Freeway heading north. "You'll scare the crap out of the first cabbie who so much as slows down for you."

"Where are we going?"

"My place. I've got a first aid kit there. And then you can tell me what the fuck is going on."

———

Tabitha lives in a Spanish-style bungalow in West Hollywood east of Fairfax. Red tile roof, weeds in the front yard. Jacaranda in bloom, its flowers an explosion of purple.

"Nice place," I say.

"It's a rental," she says as we get out of the car.

"On a waitress' salary?" I say. I'm moving a lot better. Sore as hell, but I'm not nearly as dizzy and the burning in my shoulder has reduced to a dull throb. We go in through a side entrance. The inside of the house is full of boxes, new Pottery Barn furniture, old Ikea crap. She's still moving in but she's already got some protections up on the house.

"I'm not waiting tables, anymore," she says. "I'm running Alex's bar, now."

"Really?"

"You sound surprised," she says. She goes through the house turning on lights. "Alex left it to Vivian. Left everything to Vivian, actually. She doesn't have time to run it and she wanted somebody who knew what was going on. Somebody she trusted."

Of course. I should have known when I walked into the house that Vivian hadn't bailed on her. Unless Tabitha's gotten really good in the last six months, the wards on the house aren't hers. They're subtle, misdirection spells mostly, things to make burglars think twice and to keep most supernaturals out. Hard to see, tightly woven, pack a wallop. Classic Vivian. So expertly crafted it's almost a signature.

She leads me to the bathroom and I finally get a good look at myself. My face is covered in soot and blood, cheek swollen where the demon punched me. The front of my shirt is soaked through with blood, coated in ash.

"Jesus. I look like some nightmare clown."

She pulls a towel and first aid kit from under the bathroom sink, helps me take off my jacket. It's so covered in gore she has to peel it off.

"Thinking I should have hosed you down outside first," she says. She helps me unbutton my shirt. Gasps when she sees the bruises on my chest, the bite wound in my shoulder. It's not great, but it's better than I expected. Mostly small, deep punctures where the teeth went in, but some patches of torn out flesh from where I ripped the hand off of me.

"Fuck, Eric. What happened to you?"

It's hard to see all of them among the tattoos, but I point to the bruises and contusions I can see, sounding off as best I can recall. "Punched. Punched. Jumped off a train. Punched. Bitten. I don't know what that one is. Punched. Ghost got me. You get the idea."

She soaks a washcloth, looks at the wounds and shakes her head. "I don't even know where to start," she says.

I take the first aid kit and the washcloth from her. "Let me handle it. You got me out of that store before it got really bad. Thank you. I got it from here." I shudder to think what could have happened if I'd been unconscious when the Russian finally showed up.

"But—"

"Not my first rodeo. Really. I got this."

"Okay." Relief and guilt fighting on her face. Don't blame her. "Yell if you need anything." She closes the door behind her. An hour later I'm clean, patched up and exhausted. The shower wasn't fun. My shirt's a total loss, my pants are torn in a couple spots, but they'll last until I get back to my room to change. When I come out of the bathroom Tabitha is waiting for me in the living room on the couch with her legs tucked underneath her. She tosses a t-shirt at me. "This should fit," she says. I pull it over my head. A little roomy, but it'll do.

I sit on the other end of the couch, not sure what to do next. Ask for a ride? Call a cab? It'd be bad form to steal her neighbor's car.

She reaches behind her and pulls a bottle and a couple glasses from a side table. "Remember this?" Balvenie '78.

"Was wondering what happened to that." Last I saw that bottle she'd stolen it from Alex's private stock and suggested we have a party some time. It was a bright spot in my otherwise fucked up return to Los Angeles.

"I sneaked it out of your hotel room," she says. "I figured I'd hang onto it and maybe we'd get a chance to share it. But then—"

"Yeah," I say. "But then." But then Alex died, I disappeared and Vivian . . . Vivian did whatever she did. For all my watching her I don't know what she's actually up to. I know she comes home. I know she leaves for work. I feel creepy and stalkery enough as it is just doing the occasional check on her. Everything's been at a distance. I didn't even know she'd inherited the bar from Alex. But hey, that's my M.O., right? Things get rough so I do what I do best. Run. Nobody does it better.

Tabitha opens the bottle, pours each of us a big shot.

"I don't know if I should be drinking," I say. "I need to figure out how I'm getting back to my motel."

"Eric, it's two o'clock in the morning. You're not going anywhere." She hands me my drink. "So shut up and take it."

"Yes, ma'am," I say.

She lifts her drink in a toast. "To Alex." We touch glasses and drink. It's good scotch. I only wish Alex could be here to share it.

"What happened?" she says.

"Which part?"

"All of it? Alex dying, you disappearing. Vivian says his death is your fault, and I'm still not sure what happened. Then he shows up here in my living room and screams at me that you're in trouble." She puts her glass down. "I know the world's full of freaky shit, and when I met you that got cranked up to eleven. I'm still trying to get used to it all. I mean, I didn't even know any of this was possible before a couple years ago. But the thing that I'm really having a hard time with? Your eyes."

I down the rest of my glass. "The eyes are just a reminder that I fucked everything up."

"How? How'd you fuck everything up? The hell happened to you, Eric?"

"Can I get a refill?" She pours me another. I toss it back. "Let me start with Santa Muerte."

Chapter 10

We talk until the sun peeks through the curtains. Scotch has been replaced with coffee. Tabitha has curled herself into a ball on the couch, pulled in on herself. Body language telling me getting into her car and coming here was the mother of bad ideas.

"Rough ride," she says when I've told her everything I can think of. "You know, I hadn't really believed you when you first told me about Santa Muerte. I mean, I had trouble with the whole 'seeing the dead' thing. Never would have believed you if Alex and Vivian hadn't vouched for it. But some Mexican death icon? Come on."

She takes a sip of her coffee. "But then Alex dies and Vivian tells me it's your fault, but doesn't know how. You don't return my calls. I didn't know what to believe. So after a couple of months I wrote you off. And then Alex comes screaming in here."

"I didn't call because—"

"I get it. And, to be honest, thank you. I think I'd probably have lost it if you'd shown up on my doorstep the next day with those freaky eyes. I had a lot to adjust to. Fuck, I'm still adjusting. So Santa Muerte's a real thing? Like walks and talks and all that shit?"

"Sure. Why not?"

"Because she's a fucking Mexican folktale, isn't she? I mean, I know she's not. Or at least I know that things like her are out there. Alex taught me that much. Though I never thought they were so . . . big. And Vivian's done what she can. And you might be a jerk, but I don't think you're blowing smoke up my ass. But I need you to tell me again. She's real?"

Some of the things I deal with, most mages have never heard of, much less met. Like it or not I'm in a pretty exclusive tier of the magic club. It'd be hard for even some seasoned mages to accept the things I'm saying.

And Tabitha, though she might be a talent, is new to it all. Alex was training her, trying to get her some control over her own magic. You spend a lifetime not knowing about any of this stuff and it suddenly comes crashing down on you? She's only one step removed from being normal. Still in that whole "What the Fuck" phase. Yeah, I'd be questioning things, too.

"Yes, she's real. A lot of things are real. Voodoo Loa, demons, vampires, all that shit. It might not be what you think it is, or work how you think it does, but chances are it's real. Or something very like it is real. I don't know what Santa Muerte wants or why she wants it from me, but she's real enough."

"Okay," she says. She unfolds herself on the couch, stretches and cracks her neck.

"Okay?"

"Yeah. At some point you just need to accept it, right? Whether or not you believe in a bus it can still run your ass over. But she's not your immediate problem, is she?"

"No, she's not, though I can't shake the sense that the Russian is related, somehow. And Alex showing up at the same time? That's too coincidental. Even with magic involved."

"Does seem kinda odd," she says. "Jesus, when did I get to the point where this was all just 'odd'?"

"It's a sign you're getting used to it."

"I'm not sure I want to get used to it. I grew up in Fullerton. You don't get much more white-bread than that. That's normal. That's safe. This stuff? No. This is the exact opposite of safe." She takes a sip of her coffee. "Maybe I should have stuck with the scotch."

I don't know what to tell her. To me this is normal. I've lived with this my entire life. Living with magic insulates people the way money does. We get homeschooled because, well, shit, can you imagine mages in the L.A. public schools? There's a recipe for disaster.

"I know it's scary," I say. "But this is the real world. Like it or not your eyes are open. Can't close them now."

"Speaking of which," she says, wiping her eyes with the back of her hand. She grabs a Kleenex from a box on the coffee table, wipes her nose. "Sorry. It's still a bit much. You know I used to be really close to the people

I went to high school with? College, too. Then I moved up here and I didn't talk to them much. Now I don't talk to them at all. I'm afraid to. I'm afraid to talk to people I spent my entire life with. Friends, family. What do I tell them? What do I tell them that doesn't get me committed? That doesn't put them into danger?"

"Nothing," I say. She looks hard at me, clearly not the answer she was looking for. "You just said it. You tell them this stuff you put them in danger. Hide it behind New Age horseshit if you really need to talk it out with them. Avoid coming out and saying magic. Say you're Pagan, whatever. But keep the truth away from them. It'll get them killed. Hell, the people on the train, today. They didn't know about this stuff and it killed them just as dead."

"I don't want this, Eric. I really don't want this. It scares the living shit out of me."

"Then walk away from it. You can still do that. It's not easy, but it's doable."

"Is that what you did? Tried to walk away?"

"To get away from my life here, sure, but not that. If anything it got me in deeper. I'm stuck with it. I can't get away from magic any more than you can get away from being a woman. But you're not me. You've got a little talent and you know this shit's real, but that doesn't mean you have to stay in the life. It'll stick with you. Know that. This life will try to pull you back. You won't be able to get away from it completely, but you can get some distance from it."

"What's the alternative?"

"Embrace it. You're already in a great place for that.

Vivian knows this life. She's got to have introduced you to some of the more savory people in it. Not everyone's an asshole like I am, you know."

That earns me a smile. "You're not that bad," she says, and then seems to remember she's talking to the guy with the blacked-out eyes. The smile fades. "Except you really are that bad, aren't you?"

"I try not to be, but I don't think I do a very good job."

She doesn't say anything for a long time. Distant, closed off. A minute later she says, "So, what are you going to do?"

"I don't know. At first I figured I'd just find the Russian, and, I dunno, kick his ass or something. Figured that'd be the end of it. But now? He's got Kettleman's power, he's got the knife. Who knows who else he's killed? Fucker's got a small army, though I think we put a dent in that at the hotel. I think my plan's still the same, but I need to find him before he can find me."

"How do you think he found you this last time?"

That's been bugging me since it happened, but I hadn't had time to really dig into it. "I'm not sure he was looking for me," I say. "Gabriela seemed to think he was coming back to finish her off. Who's to say that wasn't his plan and I was just at the wrong place at the wrong time?"

"But what about the Bentley?" she says.

"Yeah, that one I can't explain. Tracking me shouldn't be that easy. I need to figure out where that goddamn Russian is. It's that simple. But I don't even know his name."

"Can Alex help you? I mean, you've talked to him, right? He seems to know some things."

"So far he's shown up on his schedule. And I'm still not convinced it's actually him. He seems, I dunno, off somehow."

"He is dead."

"Yeah, but he's not like any ghost I've ever met. It's a moot point, anyway. I don't know how to contact him." She starts to say something, and stops herself. "What?"

"What about Santa Muerte?"

"Okay, I'm gonna ignore that you even said that."

"No, hear me out. I know she's all scary and shit. I mean, she scares you. Which means I'd probably pee my pants if I saw her. But she doesn't want you dead, right? She's got something in mind, but presumably you have to be alive for it. Maybe it's a good thing. Maybe you should just accept that she's there."

"We're talking about an Aztec death goddess, here. That's a big assumption. But yes, chances are she doesn't want me dead any time soon. Maybe."

"Aren't you being a little harsh? You said her husband was dead, suicide or something? Maybe she's lonely."

"You're serious?"

"You talked to her before, right? Maybe you can talk to her again? You're her—Okay, I have to confess, this weirds me out."

"What, that I'm married to her? Try being on this side of the fence. And it's not 'married.' It's . . . linked, I guess. Not quite family. Not quite employer."

"Are you sure? Because that ring's telling me something pretty different."

"No," conceding her point. "I don't know that for sure. This is kind of new territory for me. Okay, let's assume I talk to her. What then? Get even deeper in with her when she helps me out? That's a bad idea."

"I don't understand why. Maybe you need to accept it. Make it work for you. Give in. What's so hard about it?"

I stare at her a second, speechless, not believing I'm having this conversation. "Because I'm pissed off. Because she murdered my sister to get to me. I left to keep Lucy safe, to keep Vivian safe, to keep Alex safe. And she took all that time, all that effort, everything I did, and fucking burned it. She is not my friend, she's not my savior. She's a fucking monster. And this ring doesn't mean a goddamn thing other than that she's branded me."

"Okay," Tabitha says. "Okay. Just exploring possibilities is all. I understand."

"No, I don't think you do. I got to watch what she did to Lucy. I got to sit there and watch my sister's ghost reenact her murder and then be used as a fucking paintbrush to write me a message in her own blood. She doesn't get a pass. I don't know what it's going to take, I don't know how I'm going to do it, but I am going to fucking destroy her."

"Okay, I—"

"I don't know why you're trying to defend her," I say. "So stop."

"But—"

"Drop it."

"Fine. Okay. Forget I said anything. I'm sorry." She takes a deep breath, lets it out slowly. "So who else is there? There has to be someone who can help you. If this Russian guy tracked you down can't you do the same to him?"

"Tracking spells aren't my knack. I mean, yeah, I could try, but I suck at them. It's like driving stick when you don't know how. Sure, I know the theory, but the practice? I'd just as likely set something on fire."

"So find someone who can. Jesus, Eric, work with me here. You're not the only mage in town. Somebody's got to be able to give you a hand."

"Tabitha, my name is mud here. I've tried other mages, they want nothing to do with me. The only one who agreed to help me turned out to be a fake who wants to skin me alive. The last one I talked to just had her hotel burned down, probably because of me. I've tried talking to the Loa, nature spirits, the dead. Santa Muerte scares the hell out of all of them. The only things I haven't talked to around here are—" Hang on.

"What? Something just happened. I see it on your face."

"There might be something I can ask."

"That's good."

"Not necessarily. The thing I'm thinking of is . . . volatile. But it would know. That helps. Thank you." I've been dealing with figuring things out on my own for so long I've forgotten what it's like to have someone's help.

"No problem. Any other problems I can solve for you? World hunger? Climate change? Traffic on the 405?"

"Maybe. Speaking of traffic, I have to figure out how to get back to my motel. Got a neighbor you don't like whose car I can steal?"

"Guy across the street's kind of a dick."

"Perfect."

"Eric, you're not going anywhere. A few hours ago you could barely walk. Come on, sexy, you need sleep." She stands and takes my hand, tugging at it until I get up. I'm not sure where this is going, and I'm not sure I want it.

"Tabitha, I don't think I'm—"

"Me either," she says. "Sleep. That's all. But after this last night, after all we've talked about, I kind of don't want to be alone right now. Okay? Sleep."

"Sleep. Sleep is good."

We don't actually get to sleep for a good, long time.

———

Tabitha lifts her head from my chest when I startle awake, her arms and legs wrapped around me. Takes me a second to get my bearings. I've spent so much time alone that it's weird to wake up with someone else.

"Hey," she says, rubbing sleep from her eyes.

"Hey back at ya. So what happened to just sleeping?"

"You complaining?" she says.

"Not in the slightest. Just, you know, this is getting to be a habit."

She laughs. "Twice in six months is a habit?"

"Hey, cut me some slack. I don't spend a lot of time around people."

"Maybe you should," she says.

I don't know what to say to that, so I don't say anything. The silence stretches, neither of us willing to break it. I glance at the clock on her nightstand. Already late in the afternoon. "I should probably get going," I say.

"Struck a nerve?" She unwraps herself from me and rolls off the bed.

"A little, yeah." I watch her as she pads to the bathroom and flicks on the light. I'm not sure but I think she's added to the elaborate tattoo of cherry blossom branches that climb up from her hip and over her shoulder. More branches, more color.

"You get more ink?" I say, trying to change the subject.

"Couple months ago. Guy in Santa Barbara did it." She turns on the shower, pokes her head out of the bathroom. "Look, I'm not trying to make this more than it is."

"We're not talking about the tattoo, anymore, are we?" So much for changing the subject.

"We're both adults. A roll in the hay is just a roll in the hay."

"Never said it wasn't."

"We're a 'habit'?"

"Yeah, okay, not my finest moment. Sorry."

She waves it off. "As habits go I can think of worse ones. I like you. Obviously. Scary eyes and all."

"There's a 'but' in there somewhere."

"Would you date you?"

"Point." I could tell that's where she was going with

it, but it still stings. "Hey, you said you had a neighbor whose car I could steal?"

"Across the street. Yellow Hummer. Guy's an asshole. Take it with my blessing." She steps into the shower. I get up from the bed and join her.

"I'll probably dump it in the desert."

"That where you're going?"

"Yeah. The thing I need to talk to hangs out in the desert out past Cajon or Soledad Pass. Sometimes."

"You need help?"

"Thanks, but no. If things go to shit they'll go to shit fast and I'd really rather you not be in the middle of it. I like you, too, you know."

"Thanks. What exactly is it, anyway?"

"Old. Very, very old."

Chapter 11

Every year L.A. burns. Brush fires from too much heat and too little moisture sweep through the canyons, rampage down the hills. Flames chew through the landscape, an inexorable force that eats everything in its path. Thousands of people displaced, millions in property damage. All because of the wind.

Raymond Chandler called it the Red Wind. To some of the locals they're the Devil Winds. Good name for them. You know how to tell when L.A.'s about to burn? The air moves. They're the Santa Anas. Sometimes hot, sometimes cold. Always dry. They blow through the Cajon Pass, Banning, Santa Clarita. Funnel in from the desert. Set everything ablaze.

The winds blow through the streets, in through windows, cracks in doors. They go everywhere and they see everything. So if you absolutely, positively need to track something down there's really only one thing to do.

Ask the winds.

I stop at my motel to pick up a few things, get a change of clothes. When I told Tabitha what I was planning she got that same look on her face she had when I told her about Santa Muerte. One more chip out of that wall of Normal she's looking for.

I'm not entirely sure where I'm going. When I get onto the road the sun has already set. I take the stolen Hummer up the 5 Freeway and cut across the 14 toward Palmdale, tasting the magic as I crawl through traffic. The flavor shifts from the heavily Latino magic of North Hills and Sylmar to a sort of suburban kitchen-witch magic from the new subdivisions in Santa Clarita. Nothing big, nothing old.

When I get up by Vasquez Rocks it changes completely. You've seen the place in old western serials and Star Trek episodes. Massive jutting rocks angled toward the sky. Before Hollywood came knocking it was a hideout for a bandit name of Tiburcio Vasquez. And before that it was a home to local Indian tribes like the Tataviam, Chemehuevi, Serrano, Kitanemuk.

It's a tourist spot now, but you can taste all that history in the place's magic even as far out as the freeway. I get off at Agua Dulce. The park's closed, a chain running across the entrance road. I park across the street, grab a knapsack and a flashlight and draw SUPPOSED TO BE HERE in big letters across the side of the Hummer. Don't need some County Sheriff towing it when I don't have a ride back.

I haven't been to Vasquez Rocks in almost twenty years. Place is still a pit. Dry desert air, dirt and scrub brush. Nearby houses look down from the distant hills. Further out in Mojave at least you get the sense you're in the middle of nowhere. Here it feels like you're in somebody's shitty backyard.

There's a trail that loops around the park, hits that big Star Trek rock everybody's seen. Plenty other rocks like it here. High ground is good for what I need to do. There's no moon and it takes me about an hour to pick my way along the trail with a flashlight until I find a nice rise with a flat top. I climb up and start my preparations.

The evening air is cool and the wind is starting to pick up. I pull a box of salt from the knapsack and a hammer that I use to chip some stone flakes off the rock. I gather up dust from the ground, mix it and the stone flakes in with the salt. I pour the whole thing into a circle.

Now the tough part. I don't know exactly what I'm doing. I've spoken with wind spirits, Kabun, the Algonquin west wind, a handful of things that all call themselves the North Wind, but never the Santa Anas. I'm not even sure it has a proper name, or even if there's only one.

But I do know that they all talk to each other. Nature spirits are very much a part of the thing they represent and vice versa. Because of that, wind spirits tend to be a little blurry around the edges. Identities get mixed up. Boundaries don't really exist. The one I talk to tonight might just as easily have been a dust storm in China a week ago, a tornado in Ohio last month.

Fortunately, like most magic, summoning is based

on will. The chants and rituals are a way to hone in on your intent. I don't necessarily need to know the thing's name. The words don't matter. Might as well be singing Queen songs as much as chanting Vedas into the open air. It's what you've got in your head that matters most and whether or not you can channel that energy into something useful.

I sit cross-legged outside the circle. It's not a protection so much as it's a landing place. Protection against this thing is pretty useless, anyway. And if it thought I was trying to actually bind it, it'd just get pissed off.

Intent and will. Focus and power. Images in my mind of windswept deserts, blast furnace air. Fires rampaging out of control. The air scouring every living thing down to bleached bone. An hour later the wind picks up, dry and hot. Plays at my hair. Blows up little dust devils that dance around me. Another hour goes by, and another. My legs are starting to cramp up. I forgot to stretch first.

About four hours in and I feel it. A sudden presence of solid air that surrounds me, rushing past and coalescing into the circle. A dust devil six feet high flows into being with a noise of rushing wind. It pulls the dirt and mix of salt and rock that I drew for it, sucks in the dust dancing in the air.

The voice hits me from all sides. Echoes off the rocks. Talks to me, talks to itself. Sounds overlap each other, hissing like wind through trees, stripped-off bark, blowing sand.

"We are called," says one voice to my left. "We come," says another behind me. The dust devil shifts slightly, but stays rooted to its original spot. "What does it want?"

"I'm looking for someone," I say. "The wind is everywhere. The wind sees everything."

"The king asks us for help?" says a voice. "Honored," says another. "The king is dead," says a third.

"I think you've got me confused with someone else."

"It jokes." "It jests." "It makes a funny."

"Okay," I say, not liking the tone of that one bit. What king do they think I am? "I need a man tracked. Russian guy. He's killing people. Stealing their skins. Last I saw him he was in Downtown L.A. last night."

No sound but the rushing air in front of me. Silence for a long minute. Have I offended it? I sure as hell hope not. Pissed off nature spirits can be seriously bad news. I once saw a forest spirit in Canada pull an 18-wheeler down into the earth with nothing but pine tree roots.

Then, "Sergei." "He wants Sergei Gusarov." "And sister Katya."

"That's helpful," I say. I have a name. I have no idea if it's the right name, but it's a place to start. If it can help me track him even better. "Can you help me find him?"

"The king wants help." "The king needs us." "We can help the new king." The enormous dust devil pulls in on itself, particles spinning faster and faster with a sound like grinding sand, shrinking until it's the size of a dinner plate, then a softball. With a loud pop the mass solidifies into a red, glowing orb the size of my fist.

"This will find him?"

"It will glow in his direction." "It will glow brighter when he is near." "It will lead you to him."

"Excellent," I say. I don't make a move to touch it. We're not even close to done here.

"What does the king offer?" say all three voices simultaneously.

"What does the wind want?"

"Fire." "Mayhem." "Burning."

Awesome. Of course it wants fire. Flames are its plaything. All the houses ringing the canyons, the scrub brush and Joshua trees, these are all just toys to it.

"I got a Zippo here somewhere," I say. I need to stall for time as I figure something out. I need that orb if I want a chance in hell to find this Sergei guy. But I can't set off a brushfire. Twenty years ago there was nothing here. Scrub brush, empty lots. Some ranches, crazy coots living in Bucky-Dome houses in the desert. But now? Thousands of people have moved out here for cheap land. I passed half a dozen housing projects and big box stores on my way up here. A brushfire would be devastating.

"Not here." "Not this place." "Your lands."

"Uh. I live in Burbank. Sort of."

"It doesn't know." "How does it not know?" "The king does not know his own home." Then, with one voice. "Go home. Set it ablaze. Promise that and we will help you."

I am liking this less and less. I have no idea what home they're talking about, or why they think I'm a king of anything. Nature spirits sometimes speak in riddles, but this is a bit much even for the stupid ones.

But if they think I'm someone else, someone important, it might work to my advantage. I'm happy to make promises somebody else has to keep.

"Deal."

"The promise is made." "The lands will burn." "Take the sphere." I reach out and pick up the orb. All the dust and dirt that makes it up has been compressed into a smooth, polished sphere that feels like quartz. Heavy and crystalline. Deep inside I can see a faint glow on one side. I turn it this way and that but the glow stays pointed in the same direction. Southwest. Towards L.A.

"It will take time." "We know." "To claim your throne."

"I'm sure it will," I say. Especially since I'm not this king they think I am.

"A warning," one says. "Watch the false friend," it says. "Beware the dead king."

"I'll take that under advisement."

"Hunt well." "New king." "Eric Carter." And with one voice, "King of the dead."

Hot winds blow up around me, kicking up dust and dirt. I close my eyes against the blast of grit, cover my nose and mouth. A moment later the winds disappear, and all that's left is a scoured patch of rock around me and those final words in my head, chilling me to the bone.

Eric Carter. King of the dead.

Chapter 12

They knew my name. Of course they knew my name. You don't hide much from the fucking winds. Any hope that they were confusing me with someone else is gone. Wishful thinking, anyway.

I swerve the Hummer across lanes on the 14 as a truck barrels up my ass. I've been so focused on what the wind said to me that I'd completely forgotten what I'd done to the Hummer. I pull over to the side of the freeway, gravel and dust kicking up behind me. I get out to obliterate the camouflage spell I'd written on the side of the car as best I can with the Sharpie, trucks and cars barreling past me. This is almost as bad as changing a tire out here.

I get the markings erased, grab the orb and walk down the embankment. I need to clear my head, figure out what the hell is going on without worrying about getting my ass run over. I lean against a rock big enough to sit on and look up into the sky. Twenty years ago you'd see nothing but stars out here, a thick field of them away from the glare of Los Angeles proper. But now the sky is a hazy, dark blue, light bleeding up into it from all the nearby developments. The winds are already starting to pick up. I wonder if we'll get a full-on Santa Ana tonight from what I did, if the desert will burn. I hope not. It's not like the wind promised it wouldn't burn it all down. I take a deep breath of cold, desert air, try to clear my head. What the hell happened back there? What is this whole king business? There's something I'm just not putting together.

A smell of smoke and roses and a burn in the new tattoo is the only warning I get before I hear "You've had a busy night, husband." I turn and see Santa Muerte standing about five feet away, her wedding gown glowing faintly and looking in the wrong direction.

"You still can't see me, can you?"

She turns her head. "I was admiring the landscape," she says.

"Sure. What do you want now?"

"To see that you are safe. You dealt with powerful magic tonight. I would have come sooner, but," she points vaguely in my direction, "that mark you put on yourself clouds my vision."

"Then it was worth every penny. You seem awful concerned about my safety. If that's the case where were you last night when I was getting my ass handed to me?"

She says nothing.

"Uh huh. Look, I still don't know what the hell you want from me. You haven't actually given me anything to do. Vague, cryptic, 'I need you safe' shit just makes me antsy. And seriously, if you need me safe, where the fuck were you last night?" That magical Faraday cage might have kept her from sensing me, but what about after? Or before?

"You were in safe hands."

"Safe hands? Yeah, those demons were excellent hosts. I particularly liked how that little one did that whole snake jaw thing."

"You do your best to hide yourself from me and then complain that I'm not there to help," she says.

"Oh, don't get me wrong, I want nothing more than for you to fuck off and never come back. But I do want to know what the hell your game is."

"And I yours," she says. "We had an agreement and I believe you are trying to maneuver your way out of it."

"No shit. Ya think?" I show her the wedding ring on my finger, the gold glinting in the glare of the headlights speeding by on the freeway. "This I did not sign up for. Your enforcer, your assistant, whatever. Your husband? I don't fucking think so. I want an annulment."

"I think it is a bit late for that," she says. "We are linked, whether you like it or not. You know the consequences of my displeasure."

"So help me if you try anything," I say, "if you even think about hurting anyone again—"

"You spoke with the winds," she says, interrupting me. "What did they tell you?"

So she couldn't eavesdrop on my conversation with them? Interesting. I still don't know what she can and can't do. It's maddening. "They gave me the name of the man who's been trying to kill me."

"And nothing else?"

"I didn't ask for anything else," I say. "Why? Should they have?"

"No," she says. "You should take care who you listen to. Lies abound."

"So I've noticed. Are we done here? I've got to get back to town. I got some guy I need to hunt down and murder and I don't want to keep him waiting."

My phone rings. I let it go a couple times before picking up. MacFee. "Yeah." I don't take my eyes of Santa Muerte.

"Holy fuck you're alive," he says. "Wait. Is this you? Like really you? Not like skinned you?"

"Yeah," I say. "It's really me." Though I have no idea how I could possibly prove that. Or how he could prove he's him. Jesus. Talk about getting paranoid. But then I wonder who the hell would want to take Mac-Fee's skin and relax a bit.

"Oh, cool. I thought you were dead or somebody else by now. I heard about the Bruja's hotel."

"Yeah? Who told you?"

"She did. Or, her secretary did. The girl, Gabriela? Just got off the phone with her. Wanted me to get her in touch with you."

"Why didn't you just give her my number?"

"Dude. I don't just give out numbers. That's unprofessional. Anyway, she says she needs to see you. Tonight. There's a warehouse down by the L.A. river. I'll text you the address."

"So you'll give me her address, but not her phone number?" Silence. "Are you sure it's her?" I say.

"Of course. I asked her the same thing. I'm not stupid." No, but he is freaked out. MacFee's a go-to guy, not someone who lands in the thick of things.

I have no idea if Gabriela is still Gabriela or if Sergei got hold of her. There is one way to tell, though. I glance down at the orb in my hand. The glow has gotten brighter since I left Vasquez Rocks, but it's still faint. If Sergei's in the area then it should tip me off before it's too late.

"Okay. Send me the address. I'll meet her in a few hours. Hey, you spread the word about Kettleman?"

"Yeah. And people are losin' their shit. Word is that somebody tracked down the police report. I don't know how they know but I'm hearing that people are sure that the body in the morgue is his. And since some people are still seeing him walking around they're givin' him a lotta space."

"Good. If that keeps them away from him, so much the better. Might keep some of them alive."

"Yeah, well that's the good news. Bad news is that folks aren't too sure about you. You sure you didn't kill him?"

"Yes, I'm sure. No, I can't prove it. But hey, if it keeps people out of my way, that works, too. You ever hear of a guy named—" I pause. Do I want Santa Muerte to know this? Or does she already? "Sergei Gusarov?" I finally say. "Big Russian guy. Prison tats. Looks like he did time back in the mother country."

"Shit. Gusarov? Seriously?"

"So you know him? Has a sister, too. Katya."

"I know of him, yeah. He used to work for Ben Griffin as a leg breaker. Normal. No magic. Really good at breakin' legs, though. And other stuff."

"Huh. You seen him around lately?"

"No, but I heard about him a few months ago. Griffin had a bunch of Russian ex-cons working for him. Normals. Maybe a little talent here and there. Guys the mob didn't want. I don't know how, but he was able to keep 'em in line. When Griffin got killed I heard Gusarov started pulling them together to do their own thing. Then he sort of dropped off the radar."

"You hear about any of Griffin's other people?"

"Here and there. Some of them have pulled together enough that they're kinda organized. Picking up his rackets. But they're all going at it like cats in a bag. It hasn't spilled out onto the street, yet, but you know it's gonna eventually. One group takes somebody out, another takes another out. Quiet, but it's happening. From what I hear nobody really wants to get the cops involved."

"What if Sergei's playing them against each other? These are all quiet hits? Evidence left behind pointing a finger at somebody else?"

"Maybe," he says. "I don't really know. I can see if I can find out anything, though."

Yeah, this is a power grab, all right. And now that he's got the knife he can do it even better. Hell, instead of just killing somebody, he could take their skin, take over their life. Hit the right guys and he could run the rackets in the whole fucking city.

"How much?"

"I am offended," MacFee says. "This is my community. This is a threat to my well-being. I can't possibly do it for less than a thousand."

"Yeah? That on top of whatever you're billing the Bruja and me for this messenger service?"

"I'll roll that in for free."

"Nice to see some things never change. Let me know what you find out."

"On it, chief. I'll put it on your tab. Talk to you later." He clicks off.

"That was enlightening," Santa Muerte says when I hang up.

"Was it?"

"This Sergei Gusarov. I know that name. A dangerous man."

"Yeah, well he's—" I catch myself. No reason to go volunteering information. "Nothing I can't handle," I finish.

"I have no doubt. Go and take care of him. We will speak later about what the wind did or did not tell you." A breeze blows up a dust devil of sand and grit. There's that smell of cigar smoke and roses and when the air clears of dust she's gone.

A moment later my phone buzzes and a text with the warehouse address pops up on the screen. Third and Mission. That's east of the river and just off the 5. From where I am it should take me less than an hour to get there.

I don't know what happened to Gabriela after the hotel went up. It could be a trap. Only one way to find out. I make my way back to the Hummer and get back onto the freeway. All right, Bruja, let's find out if you're still you.

———

I pull off the freeway at Fourth Street. Downtown in the distance just over the bridge. Barred windows on graffitied houses, billboards advertising telenovelas, sodas, long-distance phone service, everything in Spanish. Houses give way to light commercial, the occasional abandoned storefront. Then warehouses, industrial, manufacturing. Smell of diesel from the trains across the river.

I pull up Mission and a couple blocks later look for a place to park. It's after midnight and you'd expect the only cars on this street would be trucks heading out or coming in from the train depot. But the street is crawling with them. Beat up Tercels, Maximas, Hondas. Handful of custom lowriders, kind you'd see bouncing their rear ends on Crenshaw. Couple brand-new muscle cars. They're all centered on one multistory warehouse with delivery trucks and more cars in the yard, loading docks and a top floor with lots of windows. So either I've taken a wrong turn and landed on the world's quietest warehouse party, or this is the place.

I look at the orb on the passenger seat. It's brighter, but not by much. How much brighter is it supposed to get? Like, nightlight brighter? Noonday sun brighter? When otherworldly beings hand out magical artifacts it'd be nice if every once in a while they'd include a fucking manual.

I drive around a couple of times looking for people and watching the orb to see if it gets any brighter or points toward the warehouse before I park the Hummer behind a Chevy Bel-Air halfway through a custom refit. I don't see anyone, but I don't doubt there are some guys in the top floor of the building with rifles looking out through the windows. I consider sliding over to the other side, but when I get out of the car I can see that won't work.

This is the Bruja's new place, all right. Same wards she had at the Edgewood, but these are even more impressive. Given what she ran into there I'm not surprised that she beefed up security here. I'd kinda hoped I could sneak in, but there's no way I'm getting in via the dead side. She's got the whole thing warded against ghosts, demons, constructs, probably even Scientologists and Jehovah's Witnesses. I'm not entirely sure I'll get in just walking through the front door.

Only one way to find out, I suppose. I consider drawing the Browning, but that would probably just get me shot. Instead I take the orb with me and walk toward the open gate leading to the parking lot. The orb didn't change much during my drive around the property and the glow kept pointing to the west. If it really is tuned to Sergei, he's not in there.

I stop at the open gate, energy buzzing along my skin. She's not fucking around. Some of these wards aren't just the "keep out" variety. If the wrong thing crosses the threshold they'll kill it. Here's hoping I'm on the guest list. I step into the parking lot.

And I don't explode. So that's a plus. But immediately a couple doors and the loading bays open up, and a dozen cholos with AKs pour out and surround me. They all look scared and trigger happy. I put my hands in the air.

"Gentlemen," I say. "I got an invite." One of them comes up to me to take the orb from my hand. "Try it and you're pulling back a stump." I think my eyes are helping because he backs off and rejoins his buddies covering me.

"The fuck are you, man?" one of them says. I don't recognize any of them from the hotel. Probably all those guys died.

"I'm here to talk to your boss."

"She don't talk to nobody. You want an audience, you gotta get through us."

"Jesus, are you dumbfucks serious? This is a test, isn't it? She sent you out here to see if I'd do anything stupid. To see if I'm really me. Fine." I look up at the bank of windows on the second floor. If she's watching this, she's probably up there.

"Hey. It's me," I yell. "Like really. And I know you're you. This thing in my hand? It'll track the Russian. And since I'm not getting a read from it, I know he's not here. And I got his name. Worked for Griffin. Now can you get the gangbangers to lower their guns so we can actually talk?"

No answer. The cholos are looking even more nervous. Some of them are starting to sweat. I wonder if I said boo they'd shit themselves. Or just freak out and shoot me. But god, it's so tempting.

"We're doing this?" I yell. "If I were him wearing my

skin, do you honestly think I'd be stupid enough to show up like this? Alone? After what happened in the hotel? Thanks for pulling me out of the fire, by the way. Appreciate it."

One of the gangbangers puts a hand to his ear and I can see that he's wearing a radio. "She says he's cool." Guns lower, everyone lets out a collective breath.

"I ain't scared of you," one of them says, clearly feeling the need to reassert the size of his penis.

"Then you're an idiot," I say.

Gabriela steps out onto concrete ledge of the loading bay, machete over her shoulder. "You're alive."

"More or less," I say. "I hear you—" I stop myself, wondering if any of these guys know who she is. "I hear the Bruja took out that thing that bit me."

She waves it off. "I'm done hiding," she says. "They know."

I look at the assembled troops. "So you guys know how much of a badass she is, right?" From the fact that half of them are afraid to look at her and the others are standing in rapt silence waiting for her next move, I'd say yes.

"Come on in," she says. "We've got a lot to talk about."

Chapter 13

You look like you're auditioning for a Che Guevara biopic," I say. She has bandages on her face, stitches in her forehead. Wearing Doc Martens, camo cargo pants, a black t-shirt with the words "BULLETS CAN'T HURT ME" on the front in iron-on letters.

"Yeah, just need a red beret and I'm all set," she says. "Most of my clothes went up with the hotel."

"That work?" I point to the letters on her shirt. I can't tell for sure, but I'm betting it's an extension of the kind of Sharpie magic I use. I've never gotten it to do more than fool perceptions, screw with electronics a little. Even with a camera it's more futzing with the viewer than it is the image. And I sure as hell can't stop bullets.

"More or less," she says. "Mostly it just fucks with people's aim. Helps some if I get hit. I've got other protections, though." She points at one of the tattoos peeking up over my collar. "A few of those, too. Some other things."

I follow her through a maze of shelves holding stacks of cardboard boxes, past a long empty space with a massive workspace. Long tables littered with boxes, packing materials. They're making something. But what?

"Drugs?" I say.

She gives me a look like I just farted in an elevator. "Fuck you. Knockoff handbags. Shoes. Leather jackets. Prada, Louis Vuitton. That sort of thing. Sell them down on Broadway. That's how I pay for all this shit." She shakes her head. "Drugs. Please."

"Sorry. Just seems to be a good moneymaker."

"Do I look like I'm here to make money?" No, she doesn't. She looks like someone who's trying to change the world. And from what I've seen so far she might just do that.

The second floor is mostly empty. A massive loft space with hanging barn lights. Boxes stacked on the sides. Men with rifles patrolling the blacked-out windows. She's cordoned off a space that looks like a tactical command center. Radios, computers, whiteboards plastered with maps of L.A. Guys on phones are jotting down notes, putting pins into the maps.

"I've got my crew scouring the city for this guy. You said you have a name?"

"Sergei Gusarov."

She stops, turns to look at me. "You are fucking kidding me."

"Am I like the only person who hasn't heard of this guy?"

"Probably. Guy's an asshole. He was the main reason Griffin was able to hang onto the Russians that he had. Russian mob would try to shut Griffin down and he'd send Sergei. Lots of horror stories about that guy. Effective but not smart. You sure it's him?"

"That's what the wind tells me."

"The— Okay, back up. The wind?"

"Had a conversation with the Santa Anas."

"Maybe you should fill me in a little. Let's start with after I lost you at the hotel."

I tell her what happened at the electronics store, the demons, the runes that blocked the magic. I gloss over how I got out, skip over Tabitha completely. I want to keep her out of this as much as possible. I tell Gabriela I was able to get through the door and get enough power to take the demons down.

"I figured they'd killed you," she says.

"Figured the same about you."

"Almost did. That little monster girl threw me through a plate glass window across the street."

"They leave you alone after that?"

"No, I managed to give them the slip. But I was so tapped I knew I couldn't take them. I had to cut and run. Sorry about that."

"Hey, you got me out of a burning building. More than most people would do. After I got out I tried to think of a way to track down the Russian. I suck at divination and with what he knows from Kettleman, I didn't figure casting bones was going to do it."

"Even asking the dead?"

"I thought about it, but Kettleman's ghost didn't give me a lot of hope of getting anything useful if I tracked down one of his victims. And the dead aren't real good at nuance. Asking about one guy is easy. Asking about a guy who might look like any other guy? Not much point. So I started thinking about alternatives."

I fill her in on the rest. The basics, at least. My conversation with the Santa Anas, getting Sergei's name, the orb.

When I finish she gives a low whistle. "Damn. And you're not on fire? Somebody invokes the Santa Anas and we at least get a red flag warning. I haven't even noticed a dry wind tonight."

"I kinda promised I'd burn something else. But I'm not sure L.A. won't be on fire by morning."

"It thinks you're special?"

"Something like that." From all that king business it was going on about, it sure seemed to. She gives me a look I can't quite read, like she's waiting for more. So I change the subject.

"You're not hiding behind your scary-old-witch-in-the-hotel façade," I say. "How come?"

"It's been a long time coming," she says. "I've been careful. For years. I set up the Bruja before I got out of college. Bought the hotel and built that place up from a rat-infested mess with shit plumbing and a junkie squatter in every room. I've defended it, I've fought for it."

"And now it's gone."

"And the Bruja with it. People have been poking around my operation more. Getting bolder. Last year some asshole even managed to get the LAPD onto me."

"Not another mage," I say. There aren't any hard

and fast rules about how we do things, but one thing that's pretty universal is that you don't bring in the normals. Not that there aren't mages in police work out there, but they keep that shit quiet.

"No, some lawyer on La Eme's payroll put a bug in somebody's ear. Took some doing but I got the investigation closed and then I sent the lawyer's bosses a message to back the fuck off."

"A message?"

"His head in a bag. Point is, not that long ago I didn't need to do that shit. The disguise isn't scaring people away the way it used to. So I figure with the hotel gone I gotta start over, anyway. Might as well start fresh."

"Not a simple thing to do," I say, remembering when I was forced to make a fresh start fifteen years ago. I spent a lot of months just wandering the country wondering what the hell my next move was.

"No, but I've got the same goal I've always had." She tilts her head toward the orb in my hand. "And it starts with that. You sure it'll track Sergei?"

"That's what the wind tells me. Gets brighter as he gets closer. The glow points in his direction." I hand it to her. She rolls it around in her hands, walks around the room.

"Any idea how bright it gets?"

"No clue. Probably won't know until I'm right on top of him. It's gotten brighter as I've gotten closer to L.A. but not by much. I think it's safe to assume he isn't too close."

She holds it up. The light hasn't changed the side it's on by much. "Yeah. If he were closer you'd see the light move more. He's probably pretty far out. Okay, this is good." She hands it to one of her guys tapping numbers into a laptop. Stocky Latino guy with thinning hair and a handlebar mustache. "Hey, Emilio, can you do some math on this thing?"

He takes the orb and looks it over. "You want me to see if we can use it to triangulate him? Yeah. Might need to drive around a little. Okay if I take it?"

"Sure," Gabriela says.

"Whoa, now. Hang on," I say, grabbing the orb out of Emilio's hands. "That's my only way to find the guy and it's kinda expensive. So, sorry, but I'm not about to hand it off to somebody I've never met before."

"Emilio, this is Eric," Gabriela says. "Eric, Emilio. Now you've met. Better?"

"No."

"An hour, tops, chief," Emilio says. "Seriously. Probably less. Just gonna drive around a bit with a couple of guys and map some stuff out."

"I'm gonna need a lot more convincing before I hand this thing off to anybody."

"What'd you pay for this?" Gabriela says.

"None of your goddamn business."

"Fair enough. I'm not going to ask if you trust me, but I am going to ask if you want to find this guy without having to drive all over town the rest of the night."

She has a point. I need to find Sergei and if her guy can get a fix on him quickly I might have a chance of getting him before he's on the move again.

"I'm really not comfortable with this," I say handing

it back to Emilio. "If I don't get that back I'm gonna be really pissed off."

"Duly noted," Gabriela says.

"Thanks, Chief" Emilio says and leaves with a couple of the others.

"We're on the same side here," Gabriela says.

"No, we're not. We've got some overlapping goals, that's it. But I don't know you. And you don't know me. And I'm sure as hell not part of your brave new world here. I'm sorry if I'm a little paranoid but when I run into other mages lately they have this annoying habit of trying to kill me. I'm here because MacFee said you needed to see me. So what do you need to see me about?"

She flops into a plastic chair. "I was going to share what we knew, which isn't much. Mostly where he's not. Been looking for Kettleman, but he's pretty much gone to ground. I hear from MacFee that's because of you."

"Yeah, I had him spread the word that he's dead. I hear it's helped."

"If by helped you mean anybody who sees him freaks out so he's not showing himself, sure. Nobody's seen him since the other night."

"What about the crew he had?"

"Now that we know it's Sergei, that'll be easier. I can get some names and see if we can find him that way." She drums her fingers on the table. "You know I'm not trying to kill you."

"Yeah, I know. You were, though. That kinda sticks with a guy."

"I thought you were somebody else. Look, we both have a goal here. Finding this guy and taking him down. We both have our reasons. And we could both use some friends."

I look around at everybody in the room. They're all doing things. On the phone checking on leads. Cleaning weapons. Patrolling the windows. She's got at least fifty people here.

"Looks like you got plenty of friends," I say.

"I've got a crew of normals. They've known me for years as the Bruja's secretary, right hand to some shadowy old hag in the attic who'll shrivel your balls off if you look at her funny. The minute I went public with who I really am half of them up and left. Some of them came back, and a lot of the ones who didn't are going to be a pain in my ass. And now some of the ones who are still here are starting to question me. I don't exactly have the look they were expecting. I've already had three of them try to hit on me."

"Sexism is alive and well in America. I can't imagine that went well for them."

"Once they wake up from a weeklong nap full of nightmares, they'll be fine. More or less. With the Bruja it was easy. Some old Baba Yaga witch they could be scared of was easier to swallow than a USC sociology grad. I'm starting from scratch here and I have to put the fear of god into them without her help."

"What about the vampires?"

"Bailed. Building up trust with them again is gonna be tough. I'm on tenuous ground and I don't want to see everything I've built disintegrate at my feet. Pretty soon La Eme is going to come calling again. Or the Armenians, or the Israelis, or the Chinese. I could use some friends. And I know you can, too."

"I'm doing just fine."

"Really? Bouncing from hotel to hotel, stealing cars, ex-girlfriend wants to kill you. Darius won't talk to you. Last I heard your best friend had his soul eaten and you had to shoot him in the head. Yeah, you're doing great on the friend front."

"Okay. Yes, I've burned a couple bridges."

"Burned? Dude, you napalmed the fuck out of 'em. I'm not asking for any kind of partnership, any kind of tit for tat crap. I'm just saying that we're better off being friendly with each other."

She's right, of course. I've lost a lot of people. Lost them before I even came back to town. I could use some friends. There's MacFee, but really, he's not a friend. And Tabitha . . . I'm not really sure what Tabitha is.

I stick my hand out. "I promise I won't try to kill you," I say.

She takes it and gives it a shake. "That's a start. So, what were you thinking of as a next move?"

"Use the orb to track Sergei down and feed him his own intestines. Between that and your operation here, we should be able to find him. What about Darius? Can he help?"

"When I asked him after the knife was stolen he said he didn't want to get involved and wouldn't tell me what he meant. And now the hotel's gone. The door's gone. I can't get to him."

"Why don't you—Oh. You don't know about the

other doors." That gets her attention and has me wondering what I can do with this new bonus bargaining chip.

"What other doors?"

"I think I'll hang onto that little tidbit."

"I thought we were friends."

"Promising not to kill each other isn't the same thing."

"See, this is the problem," she says. "This is why the world's so fucked up. Nobody trusts anybody. Not every mage is an asshole, you know."

"Really?" I say. "That your experience? Sure as hell isn't mine."

"Has it occurred to you that it's because you're one of the assholes?"

"I—Goddammit." She's easily as powerful as I am and she's got a small army of heavily armed thugs. I still don't entirely trust her. If I tell her where the other doors are I lose what little advantage I have. But a phrase pops into my head about how if more than three people call you a horse, buy a saddle. Whole lotta people calling me a horse these days.

"Closest one is in the last stall of the men's room in the lobby at Union Station," I say. "On the wall."

She grins. "That wasn't so hard, was it?"

"You have no idea. You need runes to unlock the door. And if you don't know what those are, I'm not showing you."

"Hey, I gave you one of my magic hand grenades. Pulled your ass out of a burning building. Doesn't that count for something?"

"Let's find Sergei and then we'll talk about it." At least this way she has an incentive not to have her people put bullets into me.

"Fair enough."

"Now I doubt Sergei's sitting around waiting for us to come for him. I still don't get what the hell he's trying to do."

"It's a power grab," she says. "And with you involved, probably a big one."

"Yeah, I get that, but there's more going on here. You said it yourself, Sergei's not that smart. Did he get smarter by absorbing Kettleman? Is this really Kettleman's plan?"

"The knife doesn't work that way. You get memories and mannerisms, and the look, sure, but it doesn't change you. Not like that, at least."

"Are you sure?" A thought pops into my head. "You've used it, haven't you?"

Embarrassment crawls across her face. "Yes. No, I'm not happy about it. I did it because I had to." She clearly doesn't want to talk about it, but I need to know what this thing can really do.

I show her the ring on my finger. Right now it's red gold with little *calaveras* etched into the surface. "Not exactly in a position to judge, here."

"Guess you're not. La Eme came at me when I was just starting the hotel. They were screwing with my people, threatening me. Whoever they threw at me I sent packing. So they send this enforcer up from Mexico, Julio Bautista. Almost killed me. I got the drop on him and I figured if I could use the knife on him I could use what he knew to keep them out of my hair."

"Did it work?"

"Yeah. He knew a lot. I fucked with their people, disrupted drug supply lines, got a bunch of them in jail, all that shit. We finally reached a truce of sorts and now we leave each other alone."

"You might be one of the scariest people I've ever met."

"Yeah, well, that worked when people didn't know I was the Bruja. I don't know what's going to happen now."

"Don't worry. You're still pretty fucking scary. So you can change into this guy? The way Sergei changes into Kettleman? That's gotta be—"

"Weird? Yes." She shudders. "Knowing what it's like to have a penis really is something I could have lived my whole life without."

"Right. Okay. I'm not sure what to do with that information. So you've got some Mexican Mafia assassin floating around in your head."

"Yes? No? Sort of? I know what he knows. Knew. Whatever. Can we talk about something else?"

"No. Though we can skip the bits about the guy's johnson. You know what Sergei can do more than I do. I hurt him when he was wearing Kettleman and when he changed back he was fine. What happens if we kill him when he's using the other skin? Does he know what Kettleman knows when he's not using Kettleman's form? Can he cast when he's back to being Sergei?" I have so many questions they all start tumbling out at once.

"It's like wearing a suit," she says. "It doesn't change you, it just sits on top of you. Makes what you say come out the way that person says it. Mannerisms, facial tics, that kind of thing. Julio only speaks Spanish, for example. I can understand English when I'm him, but I can't speak it. So Sergei knows what Kettleman knows when he's being Kettleman. Other times, it's like trying to remember something you read in a book. And he can't cast. At least I can't cast when I'm wearing Julio."

"What about getting hurt?"

"I'm not sure. I've only been hurt once when I was wearing Julio and that was the last time. Hurt like a sonofabitch, but when I switched back to me I was fine. I haven't tried going back. That was about four years ago."

"When Sergei showed up at the hotel as Kettleman he looked fine," I say. "So maybe the skin heals when you're not wearing it?"

She shrugs. "I don't know what to tell you. Julio took a double-barreled twelve-gauge to the abdomen. I'm not about to try him on again to find out." Can't blame her for that. Something about how this whole thing works is gnawing at me.

"This knife belongs to some corn god?" I say.

"God of agriculture, Xipe Totec, and that's just one possibility. There are a lot of others. Tezcatlipoca, maybe. He's a trickster, the whole taking on a skin to disguise yourself thing fits. Or Huitzilopochtli. Sun god who demanded human sacrifices. Could be any of a dozen different ones. Could be none of them. Could have been made by some guy a couple thousand years ago and a story got attached to it. Why?"

"Let's assume Sergei's too stupid to do this on his own," I say. "And let's assume he's coming after me as some sort of Santa Muerte power grab."

"Oh, I don't like where your brain is going with this," she says.

"Me either," I say. "What if our shot-caller's another god?"

Chapter 14

"That is so not something I want to think about," Gabriela says.

"I'm not crazy about it, either, but how did Sergei know about the knife? How does anybody know about the knife? It's been hidden in your family for generations. He didn't just stumble on it."

"People can find these things, you know," she says. "There are stories about it. Do enough detective work and you can find anything."

"You honestly believe that?"

"It's better than thinking I'm stuck in the middle of a divine pissing match. Look, it's not that I don't believe it can't be another god—"

"It's that you don't want to believe."

"No, I don't," she says. "Know why? Because I can do fuck-all about it. Say you're right. What do we do? Kill Sergei? You think that'll end it?"

"You think it'll end it if it's another mage behind it?"

"No, but a mage is just another person and I can kill

another person. Look, I don't know if you're right or not, and I really fucking hope you're not, but I don't think it matters right now. Look at it this way, if we take down Sergei, it might flush out whoever is behind it into the open. And if we're wrong and it's Sergei working on his own, then problem solved."

Can't fault that logic. "So we table that. Still need to find him."

"I can help with that." Emilio comes up the stairs with the orb in one hand and a laptop in the other. "So we drove around a while with a GPS and I plugged data into this mapping software and—" He looks at our blank faces, rolls his eyes. "He's in Koreatown."

"Oh, that's not good." It could just be a coincidence, but my gut tells me it's not.

"Why?" Gabriela says.

"That dead friend who showed up at the hotel to warn me about the attack was Alex Kim. He used to own a bar in Koreatown. Had an Ebony Cage under the floorboards that he was siphoning magic from and bottling."

"I know the place. I used to buy from him every once in a while. Stuff's handy to have around. Always wondered how he did it. You think Sergei's after the cage?"

"Don't know. But the fact he's in K-Town's awful coincidental. If he is and he gets hold of it, that could be a problem. With that much power at his fingertips and Kettleman's knowledge, there's no telling what he can do with it." And if he is after the cage then it puts a new spin on the woman who came after me on the train. Maybe she wasn't tracking me. Maybe she was checking the bar out and I happened to be in the wrong place at the wrong time.

Gabriela turns to Emilio. "You know where in K-Town?" she says.

"Somewhere around Wilshire and Normandie or thereabouts. Give or take a few blocks."

"That's the bar, all right. I'd bet on it." I pull out my phone, punch Tabitha's number. The bar doesn't close for another hour. She might be there working.

"We can't throw everybody at him," Gabriela says. "Not in public. But we can come close. Emilio, I want twenty guys, five cars. Make sure everybody's got a radio and an AK. We'll have a few go inside and the rest will wait outside in case he gets out."

"We are not going in there with guns blazing," I say. Tabitha's phone goes to voicemail. I think about leaving a message, but if Sergei really is there and he's gotten to her, she might already be part of his skin suit collection. The thought makes my stomach turn and I shove it back into the corner of my mind that it crawled out of. I hang up without saying anything.

"If we miss him—"

"Bar's still open," I say. "There are still people there. You think he's going to look like himself? Or like Kettleman? When he knows people are looking for him now? Who are you going to shoot? Everybody? No. Besides, there might be people I know there and I'd really rather they not get hit."

"If he's there they might already be dead. The knife doesn't take long to work. It's not like skinning an animal. Just a few cuts and it's all over. Five minutes, tops. We have a better chance of ending this if we do shoot everybody."

"Now who's the asshole?" I say. "Compromise. Same plan, but just you and me go in. You'll have people on radios outside. We find him, you tell them what he looks like. When we flush him out they take him. When this goes down you know the cops are going to show pretty goddamn fast. This gives your crew a better chance to get away. You're out of the closet now, Bruja. They get picked up, you have a lot more to lose."

I can tell she wants to argue with me, but that last bit stops her. Even if her homeless vampires knew, even if some of the magic set knew, her biggest defense was still hiding behind the Bruja. Kept her safe from the normals, at least. If things got hairy the Bruja could conveniently die. But now that she's come clean she's got no buffer. It's her people who are going to keep her alive more than anything else.

"Emilio," she says. "Cut that down to two cars and eight people. Have them follow us to the bar."

———

I didn't think it was possible, but the bar is even more garish at night than it is during the day. Neon lights and flashing bulbs. It looks more like a strip club than any kind of regular bar. I miss the all black on black it used to be. Had a seedy dive feel to it. But this, Jesus, it's an assault on the eyeballs.

"The place certainly is . . ." Gabriela pauses as she

searches for a word, comes up short, and settles on, "something."

"Ain't it just?"

"Is it as bad on the inside?"

"I have no idea. It was a lot more goth the last time I was inside. How's the orb doing?" I say. The cars with Gabriela's men behind us split off and take up positions around the bar.

"Lit up like a fucking Christmas tree," she says, showing it to me. One side of it glows a deep amber, shifting as we pass the bar. He's in there, all right.

We park a block away. Bar doesn't close for another half hour but most of the crowd's let out already. I check the Browning, make sure a round's chambered. Gabriela pulls out the machete.

"So we're not going for the subtle approach then?" I say.

"The minute we walk in there he's going to know," she says. "Probably has other people inside, too. I'd really prefer it if you'd just let me blow the place up."

"That's an even worse idea," I say. An Ebony Cage is made out of living demons, their bones twisted and wrenched into impossible shapes. Who knows how long these ones have been trapped in it? "You ever seen an Ebony Cage break? That thing so much as cracks we're going to have worse things to worry about than a crazy Russian with a knife."

"That bad?"

"You want a bunch of pissed off demons running rampant through K-Town? I sure as hell don't want to have to clean up that mess."

"Let's get this over with then."

It's only been a few months since I've been inside but it feels like a lifetime ago. The charms and wards Alex installed in the front door to help ease bar patrons into spending more money and not starting fights are still carved into the doorjamb. I can feel their telltale buzz against my skin as I step through. The bouncer I saw last time I was here is gone, but there's an empty stool by the door for him.

The inside of the bar isn't any better than the outside. I'm assaulted by a blast of K-Pop coming through wall speakers, dance videos playing on monitors scattered throughout the room. The clientele used to be older, more sedate. Tabitha and Vivian have really gone out of their way to pull in a younger crowd. Though the evening is winding down, some of them are still dancing in the middle of the room while a couple of bored bartenders handle last call. Most of the customers are Asian, and none of them look like they're part of Sergei's crew. Too young, too drunk, too pretty.

The layout of the bar is mostly as it used to be, multiple bars and stages all pointing toward the center of the room. But the chairs and tables are arranged differently. Before they'd been bolted down to keep them in place, to enforce a kind of Feng Shui to funnel the emotional energy of the bar patrons toward the Ebony Cage for the demons to feed on. Later, Alex could siphon off the magic they pissed out and sell it by the bottle. Now they're just regular chairs and tables, no sign that they're designed for anything other than sitting in.

"The cage isn't here," I say.

"What? You sure?" Gabriela says.

"Layout's changed. Alex had it specially designed. So either they've moved the cage or did a remodel without realizing it was important. And I know for a fact that they knew about it. At least Vivian did."

"Focus," she says. "We're here for Sergei. Cage isn't our problem." She looks down at the orb, moves it a little. "That way," she says, pointing to a hallway next to the main bar.

"There's an office and a storage room back there," I say. "And a back door." Knowing Sergei is here and not knowing where has me jumpy, but there's something else about this that's bugging me and I can't place it.

"Okay," she says. "Emilio, you get that?"

"I got it," Emilio says over the radio. "We got a car in the back and we're pulling another into the lot. Anybody comes through what do you want us to do?"

"Don't suppose I can just shoot them?" she asks me.

"I'd rather you didn't."

"Keep them from leaving," she says. "If they look like they'll be a problem then shoot them."

"Got it," Emilio says.

"Notice there's no bouncer?" I say as we head toward the back. "That strike you as a little odd?" I half expect one to step out of a corner and stop us on our way to the back, but it doesn't happen. Even the two harried bartenders are so focused they don't notice us going back there. At the office door Gabriela shows me the orb. Bright as a flashlight and the glow is very clearly pointing at the door. I can't hear anything inside over the music coming from the bar.

Neither one of us wants to set off a spell just yet and alert him, but I've got a shield in mind ready to fire off. I draw the Browning and put my hand on the doorknob. Gabriela lifts the machete high over her head.

"Do me a favor and don't take my head off with that thing," I say.

"No promises," she says. I throw the door open, stepping aside so Gabriela can run in past me. Tabitha's sitting behind her desk, a man standing next to her. I've seen him before. He was the bar's bouncer when Alex ran the place.

"Eric?" Tabitha says. "What are you doing here?"

The glow in the orb is a white hot point, clearly singling out the bouncer as Sergei. And if that wasn't enough, the minute Gabriela gets past me he changes. I expect the Russian's face and prison tattoos, but instead he throws off the bouncer's form and changes into Kettleman as easily as a dog shaking off water.

Tabitha jumps out of her chair in surprise when her bouncer turns into a sixty-year-old man, his clothes hanging on him like a scarecrow.

Gabriela swings the machete down at him, but he pivots at the last second and the blade swings through empty air. He brings a fist up and I think he's going to try to punch her, but as it gets near her a red glow springs up around it and ropes of light wrap themselves around her. Her arms are pinned, the machete useless at her side. He follows up with a knee into her abdomen and she doubles over. The orb falls from her fingers and shatters on the floor like a snow globe.

A lance of fire snaps out of his fingers at me. I duck

to the side and the door behind me explodes into splinters. He changes tactics and grabs Tabitha. The glow around his hand intensifies.

"Can you shoot me before I kill her?" he says.

"I'm willing to give it a try," I say, but I know I'm not. There's no way I'm going to make that shot before he can kill her, and if I miss there's no way I won't hit her.

"What the hell is going on, Eric?"

"It's all good," I say. "I'll get you out of this."

"Really? Let's find out," he says. He steps from behind the chair towards me and the door, dragging Tabitha in front of himself like a human shield.

"Let her go and I won't kill you," I say.

"You fucking better," Gabriela yells from the floor. "Otherwise I sure as hell will."

"Seems the young lady disagrees with you," Sergei says. "How about you, dear?" he says to Tabitha. "Do you think he should take his shot?" It occurs to me that I've never heard Sergei speak as himself. I wonder what he sounds like when he's not wearing somebody else's skin suit.

"Eric, what is this?" Tabitha says. "Who the hell is this person?"

"It'll be fine," I say. "We're working this out." I back away to make room for him to pass. I still have my gun on him, but I don't trust myself not to hit Tabitha. He backs through the door, Tabitha still between us.

"I'm very sorry about this, dear," he says. "But I can't have Mister Carter following me. I'm sure you understand." He shoves her away from him. She stumbles, starts to run toward me and he lets loose a lance of fire from his fingers that hits her in the back, blowing a basketball-sized hole out through the front of her chest.

I freeze. Everything slows to a crawl. Tabitha standing in front of me, her chest a blown-out cavity, drops to the floor, gasping for air that won't come, blood and flesh, bits of bone spraying out in front of her, covering my shirt, spattering my face. I can see shredded bone, pulped meat, destroyed organs. I can smell the stink of burnt flesh. My vision narrows until all I can see is her lying on the floor in front of me, face down with a hole in her you could drive a truck through.

"Goddammit, he's getting away," Gabriela yells. Sergei morphs into his own body, his clothes too tight around him, and bolts down the hall. The spell holding Gabriela in place evaporates and she scrambles to go after him.

Time rushes back in like a dam breaking. I run to Tabitha, fall to my knees. Blood is spreading across the floor in one long, steady flow, the heart that should be pumping it completely destroyed. I can't think of what to do. I turn her over. Her eyes are blinking, mouth working as she tries to pull in air to fill lungs that aren't there anymore. Part of my brain wants to try to shove all the blood back in. Another part wants me to try CPR, but there's no chest to do compressions on, no heart to start.

"I need help here," I say. Tabitha grabs my hand, not quite dead, yet. She hangs onto it as tight as she can, eyes going in and out of focus, body shaking as it tries to suck in oxygen it'll never get.

Gabriela looks at Tabitha on the floor. Shakes her head. "There's nothing to do, Carter. I am not letting him get away." She runs after Sergei.

When Tabitha dies, she's gone. Her hand loosens in mine. The light fades from her eyes and it's all over. She doesn't leave behind a ghost. A lot of people don't. She's off to wherever it is she's supposed to go. Dead. Like my parents, like my sister, like Alex. She's gone.

And I am not going to let that fucking happen.

I know rationally that Gabriela's right. There's nothing I can do, but I keep going through every spell I know, anyway. I've got nothing. My magic doesn't heal. I can't stitch people up or put their hearts back together or mend broken bones.

But as I'm trying to remember every little trick I ever learned, anything that might help, something inside me perks up. That dark power I felt in the electronics store with the demons. For whatever reason it's awake and I have its attention. I don't know what it is. I don't know what it can do, but it's alive and inside me and it wants out.

"All right, you sonofabitch. Let's see if you're good for anything besides killing."

I feel that same rush of power pulse through me. My chest explodes into pain. I push past it. My insides feel like they're being torn apart. This is worse than in the electronics store or on the train. My vision blurs, goes black around the edges. For a second I wonder if this thing inside me has decided that the best way to save her is to kill me.

No such luck. I can feel the power flow out through

my hands and eyes into her corpse. Muscle knits beneath my hands, bones stitch themselves back together. The ravaged hole Sergei's spell made through her closes up. Skin closes over new muscle. A second that feels like an hour goes by. As she heals it feels like my insides are being torn apart. I hang on and keep pushing. Then I feel a heartbeat in her chest. She rears up from the floor, gasps for air. Then falls back, unconscious. But she's breathing.

In the distance I hear gunfire, Gabriela yelling orders to her men through the radio earpiece. Screams inside the bar as it empties out in a panic. Explosions.

A few seconds later Gabriela runs back into the office. "We have to go," she yells at me. "No fucking thanks to you he got—" She stops as she sees Tabitha lying on the floor. Alive.

"That—What the hell did you do?"

"I don't know." My breath is coming out in ragged gasps. The pain in my chest subsiding, more quickly than in the storage room, but slower than I'd like. I just hope it was the right thing to do.

I've animated corpses, made puppets of dead meat dance. But I've never done this before. I didn't know I could. And considering what I used to make it happen, I'm not entirely sure I'm the one who did it.

Gabriela stares at Tabitha breathing on the floor, no evidence of the massive hole that went straight through her. Gabriela snaps herself out of it, grabs my shoulder. "Come on. We have to go," she says. "Cops'll be here any second."

"I'm not going anywhere." I get up, wipe blood

from my hands onto my pants, pick up the Browning from the floor.

"We can't be here when the cops show."

I pull a nametag and a Sharpie from my coat pocket, write the word COP on the tag, blood from my fingers coating the edges. Pump some juice into it and slap it to my chest. "You can't be here. I need to be here."

"Jesus, they'll take care of her."

"And I need to make sure that happens. She needs, fuck I don't know what she needs, a hospital probably. I'm not leaving her alone."

Gabriela chews the bottom of her lip. "Then you better see this. That nametag's gonna do you fuck-all if you can't explain what just happened out back. Come on." I follow her out to the parking lot. Most of the cars are on fire. The explosions I heard. A couple near the back, a Honda and Tabitha's Mini Cooper are fine.

"The fuck did he do?"

"Sergei turned back into Kettleman once he hit the parking lot. My guys opened up on him, but he chucked a fireball and did that to them." There's no way there's anyone left alive in those cars. It's like a bomb went off in each and every one of them. Sergei pulled out all the stops.

"You froze," she says, eyes accusing. "We fucking had him and you froze. Who the hell is that in there, anyway?"

"Her name's Tabitha. She runs the place. She's a friend. I'm sorry."

"A friend? I lost eight people. Eight loyal people. Because you fucking got sentimental." She presses the heels of her palms into her eyes. "Fuck!"

"We'll find him again."

"Yeah? And who will he be this time, huh? And how are we going to track him down without your fucking little gadget? How many more people am I going to lose if we do find him? They trusted me. They trusted me to keep them safe."

Sirens whine in the distance. "I'm not staying," she says. "Good luck with the cops."

The police will be here any second now, and once people realize nothing else is going to explode the lot's going to fill up with looky-loos. Gabriela walks to a Lexus parked on the street. She snaps her fingers and it chirps as it unlocks for her.

"Your people knew full well what they were getting into," I say. She's not the only one pissed off about this. "Or do they just like carrying guns because it looks cool?"

"Fuck you," she says. "They were my responsibility."

"And Tabitha is mine."

"Well, at least you got to save her. I've got eight charred corpses sitting in a goddamn parking lot. And the fuck did you do in there, anyway?"

"I told you, I don't know. It just . . . happened."

"This was a complete clusterfuck," she says. "And right now all I want to do is shove this machete so far up your ass it knocks out teeth," she says. "So I'm leaving. If you manage to talk your way out of this call me. And then I'll figure out whether or not to fucking kill you." She gets into the Lexus, slams the door, peels out into the street.

I head back inside to Tabitha. She's breathing, seems fine. Just out cold. My hands are shaking, the blood on them has taken on a dark, metallic sheen. I can feel it drying on my face. I have no idea if she's going to be okay.

I pull up a chair and wait for the police to arrive.

Chapter 15

When the cops show it doesn't take much to convince them I'm one of them. A little "these aren't the droids you're looking for" and some Sharpie magic can work wonders. I get some weird looks for wearing sunglasses in the middle of the night, but nobody says anything. The paramedics are confused as fuck. Tabitha's clothes show what looks like a gunshot, there's blood all over the place, bits of meat and bone, but she's got no wound. They don't know what to do with her, so they haul her into the back of an ambulance.

"Is she going to be okay?" I say, getting in behind them.

Paramedic shakes his head. "Everything scans. Heartbeat, blood pressure, O_2, it's all fine. Don't know why she's out, though. Could be anything. Drugs, trauma. We'll know more when we get her to the ER. She should be fine."

That right there is the problem. She should be fine. She should be awake and moving and generally pissed off at having been shot. But she's not and I'm starting to get worried. I can think of half a dozen things worse than being dead and I have no idea what I actually did to her.

"You know her?" the paramedic asks.

I almost say yes, and it's my fault she's like this, like everything's my goddamn fault. But then I remember I'm supposed to be a cop and say, "No, never seen her before."

"Boy howdy, was that unexpected," Alex says from the passenger seat of the ambulance. He leans back to look at Tabitha, whistles. "Nice job patching up the hole, though."

"The fuck do you want?" I say. The paramedic looks at me, frowning.

"Nothing," he says. "Are you okay, detective?" he asks.

"Oooh, detective," Alex says, clapping his hands. "Are we playing cops and robbers now?" He makes finger guns at me and "pew pew" noises. I don't say anything, don't even look at him.

"Are we not talking anymore? You're gonna hurt my feelings," he says. "And here I thought I had graduated from hallucination to friend."

"Sorry," I say to the paramedic. "Where are you taking her?"

"Straight to Hell is my guess," Alex says.

"UCLA Westwood," the paramedic says. "We'll be there in a few minutes." I've done what I stuck around to do. They've got her ID, they'll get her squared away. There's nothing more I can do for her. We're a few blocks out from the bar, far enough, I think.

"Oh, a hospital," Alex says. "Yeah, that'll fix her right up. Only, wait. No, it won't. She's gone, son. Been gone a long, long time." He laughs. "Oh, man. This is so fucked up. You have no idea."

"The fuck are you talking about?"

"Sir?" the paramedic says.

"I'd love to tell you," Alex says. "Can I?" He cocks his head like a dog figuring out if it can eat the cat. "No. I don't think I can tell you that one. Rules. I hate rules. So many pissy, little rules."

That's it. I've had enough. "Pull over," I say.

"Excuse me?" the paramedic says.

I draw the Browning, shove it in the paramedic's nose. "I said pull. The fuck. Over." The driver hits the brakes. The ambulance skids to a stop, everything in the back lurching. I push the back door open and jump out. "Now get her to the hospital, or I'll fucking hunt you down and kill you."

The driver hits the gas, leaving me standing in the middle of Wilshire Boulevard waving a gun, what little traffic there is at three in the morning backing up behind me. Some guy in a Porsche revs his engine, lays on his horn.

So I shoot out his windshield, put a couple rounds into his passenger seat. The driver goes white and if he hasn't pissed his pants I'll be impressed.

"Wow. You are an angry, angry man," Alex says.

"Gotta shoot something," I say. "And not much

point in shooting you." I point the gun at his head. "Or is there?"

"If you want to hit the tree behind me, sure. Hey, here's an idea, how about we take this someplace that isn't the middle of the street? Or would you like to talk more in jail?"

"You know what I did to her. You know what that power is that I drew on. I want some fucking answers. Who are you? What are you not telling me?"

Traffic is building up behind me. A couple brave souls have slowly edged past me, staring at me as I rant and wave the Browning around, headlights throwing wide shadows across the street. To them I'm just one more crazy fucker with a gun. They can't see Alex. The Porsche driver tries to move the car and I stop him by pointing the gun at him.

"Lots, really," Alex says. "For your own good."

"Mine, or yours? You know what, forget it. You won't answer me, I know somebody who will." I go to the driver's side of the Porsche, my gun never wavering from the driver's head. He locks the door, but I pop it with a snap of my fingers and yank it open.

"Out. Now." The driver tumbles out, throwing his wallet and watch at me. Asking me not to kill him. I look at the surprisingly dry seat before I slide into it.

"You have remarkable bladder control," I say. "Be proud of that. Now get the fuck out of here." I gun the engine, leaving the traumatized driver crying in the street.

"You're thinking of going to see Santa Muerte, aren't

you?" Alex says, appearing in the bullet-filled passenger seat next to me. "You don't want to do that."

"I don't want to do that or you don't want me to do that?" I say. "I haven't seen the little lady in a while. I'm sure she's worried sick about me. I'll pop on by, have a few laughs. Introduce you to her. Whatta ya say? Something tells me she'd just love to meet you."

"You know, I don't like you when you're angry," he says. "You get all sarcastic."

"Then tell me what's going on."

"How about I show you instead? This is a good spot for it. Park the car."

We're just coming up on Hancock Park and the La Brea Tar Pits. I pull the Porsche over. Alex is gone before I even pull the key, but I can see him inside the park, just on the other side of the fence. I have to climb over it to get to him.

"Lovely place, isn't it?" he says. We're at the edge of the Lake Pit, the park's largest pool of liquid asphalt. Life-size mammoth statues, two adults and a baby, posed to recreate a grim scene. An Ice Age memento mori of fiberglass and cement. One of the adults is trapped in the tar, its mate and child bellowing from the shore.

"Yeah, it's a hoot." The tar pits are as much cemetery as death trap. Forty-thousand years ago everything from dire wolves to mammoths to giant sloths were trapped in the tar, stuck until they died of dehydration or were torn apart by predators, who quickly found themselves trapped as well. Nothing's died here in a long, long time, but I can feel it anyway, thick and fetid. A sense of death and desperation as the animals panicked and died.

"I think so," Alex says. "Did you know that there are pits all around Mexico City, some of them just now being rediscovered, some that are never going to be found. Pits from before it was Tenochtitlan, a city on a lake. Before the Aztecs, before the Toltecs. Full of skulls. All of them the lives that the sun god Huitzilopochtli demanded before he even had a name. All so that he would rise in the east the next morning to keep the darkness at bay a little while longer. Hundreds, thousands of sacrifices. So many dead and your scholars have no idea. They think they do, but nothing compares to the reality. And we know how that turned out, don't we? A dead civilization marked by mass graves that no one will ever see."

He turns to me, spreads his arms out wide. "Like this place. How many dead are here, Eric? I know you can feel them. They're old, buried, but they're not gone. All those animals who wandered too close, who died of starvation, fear. Thousands upon thousands upon thousands of dead. There might not be a bigger death pit in all of California."

The ground trembles and I think we're having an earthquake. A hole opens in the ground next to me, widens, deepens. I jump away from it, expect it to fill with a geyser of liquid asphalt, thick tarry oil, to pull me down and leave me to rot like the animals that died here thousands of years ago. Instead dirt and soil keep disappearing, deepening the pit. Wide, flat stones burst from the sides, click together. A spiral staircase descending into the darkness.

Alex starts down the stairs. "You wanted answers, necromancer," Alex says. "Come on down and get them."

Chapter 16

"You're fucking kidding me, right?" I say. "You want me to go with you down into a pit that just magically appeared in the ground?" I kick a rock over the side of the pit. It bounces off one of the stone steps and disappears into the darkness. I don't hear it land. "Oh, and bottomless, too? You just really pulled out all the stops. Where's my skullcap? Do we get torches?"

"Allow me some mystery," Alex says. "Jackass."

"Why are you even walking? You don't need to walk." He answers me with a raised middle finger. The darkness swallows him up. I cannot believe I'm actually considering this. I stand there, weighing my options. Follow and maybe get buried alive, maybe get some answers, or stand out here with my dick in my hand and get bupkes. The police sirens in the distance decide it for me. They're going to find that Porsche in about two minutes.

"I know I'm gonna regret this," I say, pulling out my phone and using it to light the steps. I follow him down into the pit.

"I guarantee it," Alex yells up from below me. He sounds far off, but he shouldn't be more than a few yards ahead of me. A few circles down and the light above me fades. I look up and see the opening hundreds of feet above me, when it should only be a couple dozen feet at the most. Not long after the cool night air becomes drier, hotter, the moisture disappearing like it's being sucked out by a vacuum cleaner. I keep walking, using my phone to light the way. I know I've only been walking a few minutes but it feels like hours.

"And here we are," Alex says, as I hit the last step. "My humble abode. Ta-da!"

I step off the last stair into darkness so complete the paltry glow from my phone can't penetrate it. My feet clatter against something on the floor and I freeze. No telling what he's got down here.

"Impressive," I say. "And, you know what? A little dark. A light would be awesome." A soft glow rises along the walls and I find myself in a long chamber carved out of stone. The walls are rough-hewn volcanic rock. I click off my phone and slide it back into my pocket.

The floor is littered with skeletons. I stop counting corpses after I hit thirty. Bits of cloth and dried skin hang off them like cobwebs. Some with weapons, some with armor. All pointed in the same direction. They died trying to get to the far end of the room. Even if none of them left ghosts I should feel something. Some kind of twinge that tells me this is a mass grave. But there's nothing here. I bend down to pick a helmet off of one of the skulls.

"Nice décor."

"You like?" Alex says, shuffling his feet through the piles of bones like a kid in a ball pit, his feet passing through the bones as if they weren't even there. "I call it Early Spanish Conquistador."

I follow him to the far end of the room, stepping around bones as best I can. He stops at a jade statue of a man sitting cross-legged on the ground. Gaunt, with wiry muscles, his ribs showing, his belly empty with the outlines of organs pressing against the flesh. Though his head is a bare skull, there are eyes in his sockets that seem to cast an intensity of anger that's palpable. He's wearing an elaborate headdress adorned with feathers, a necklace made of eyeballs. Stunning workmanship. Everything from the grinning skull face to the headdress to the loincloth between his legs seems to be carved from an entire block of jade.

"You know that marriage deal you've got with Santa Muerte?"

"How could I forget it?"

"I'm the ex-husband."

It takes a few seconds for it to sink in. I crouch to get eye level with the angry-looking statue sitting on the floor. I've seen these designs before in other statuary, these different elements sculpted and carved by clumsier hands. As if those others were desperately trying to capture the essence of this thing right here. And then I realize that they were.

"Mictlantecuhtli. This isn't a statue. This is actually you. The King of Mictlan." The things the wind told me are beginning to sound a lot more worrisome.

"I'd give you a cigar but, well, if you can find one in this mess you're welcome to it."

"Where are we?" I say.

"Not under the La Brea Tar Pits, I can tell you that."

There's a familiarity to all this. It's not the Conquistadors, the statue, or even the cave. It's the dry air that smells of dust and locked-up rooms, the feeling that the world's been hollowed out and left to stagnate. I felt that before in the vision I had of driving with Alex in the Eldorado.

And before that when I visited Santa Muerte's realm. "This is Mictlan," I say.

"More Mictlan-adjacent. A subbasement of Mictlan."

"I heard you were dead. Committed suicide."

"Suicide's maybe not the word," he says. "My choice and I'm dead, but gods don't die like people die. It's more like sleeping. You don't kill an idea, but sometimes you can bury it pretty damn deep. When the Spanish came they took everything. Slaughtered my people with their ideas and words as much as they did with their swords. But we gave them syphilis, so you know, there's that. But I got tired and people stopped believing. Or maybe it was the other way around, I don't know. So."

"So you came here to die? And this is what happened to you?"

He points to the carpet of bones. "Some of the Spanish figured out how to break into Mictlan. They figured they'd rape the heavens the way they raped the land. Did a number on the place. Chased me down and I brought them here. They realized too late it was a trap. Their souls are still wandering around here somewhere."

"And your wife, Santa Muerte?"

"I hate that name," he says, spitting the words out. "She used to have such a beautiful name. Mictecacihuatl. A proud name. Powerful. What is she now? Some third-rate saint for a religion that won't even acknowledge her. Some peasant goddess who has to hide herself behind the trappings of her conquerors."

He fixes his eyes on mine and I can feel a burning hatred coming from him. "And she's not my wife, anymore," he says. "She's yours."

"That was not my idea. I was railroaded."

"Doesn't matter. Point is you're married to her now. And I wasn't even invited to the wedding. What do you know about the King of the Dead?"

"There are a lot of them," I say. Gods like to think they're the only game in town, but when you've got all of human history to work with they tend to stack up on each other. "I've met a couple. Used to hang with some of the Ghede Loa. Samedi, Cimetiere."

He laughs. "Those aren't kings. Shepherds and keepers, maybe. Protectors and judges. But kings? Please. Compared to Mictlantecuhtli they're nothing."

"What's with the switch from first person to third?" I say. I think I know, but I want to confirm it.

"Because Mictlantecuhtli is a name and a title."

He lets me chew on that, watching me, not talking. My mind grabs onto that idea and worries it like a dog with a rat. The entity is the title. The title is the entity. The king is dead, long live the king. Magic is based on belief and belief takes that shit seriously. It's like a logic puzzle by M.C. Escher. None of the conclusions have to make sense, they just need to be logical. The pieces start to click into place.

He's Mictlantecuhtli. Mictlantecuhtli is the King of the Dead. The King of the Dead is the husband of Santa Muerte. I'm the husband of Santa Muerte. And if I'm the husband of Santa Muerte then I'm—

"Fuck me."

"We have a winner!" He throws his arms wide into the air. "Welcome home, O Lord of Mictlan!"

The power I tapped into on the train, that I used to kill those demons Downtown, that I used to heal Tabitha. This is where it came from. It's his power, now mine. Except—

"There's two of us," I say. "If I'm the Lord of Mictlan then what are you? Why can't I use that power when I want it? It comes and goes."

"I've always been around, but constrained. Watching the world go by. Observing things. But when you married Mictecacihuatl I— woke up isn't entirely right. Became aware of you? Something like that. You're becoming more like me, I'm becoming more like you. You're being rewritten on a cosmic scale. We both are. That's how I'm able to appear to you, how I can pluck bits and pieces from your head."

"That's how you know about Alex," I say.

"That and how I can appear to you at all. And also how I managed to get past that funky new tattoo you got. I was already in the house before you locked the door, so to speak. Sometimes I can show up, other times— there's interference. I'm not sure from where but I can guess. Point is, we've got a link to each other. I can't read your thoughts but I can pull enough to get an idea of what's going on."

"What about your power? Is that interference, too? Is that why I can't use it all the time?"

"That's just time. It's early days, yet. Right now all you can do is touch it. The fact that you can use it at all right now is not a good sign for you."

I start to ask why, but I already know the answer. I don't get the whole package until I'm completely him. What the wind told me makes sense now. Calling me the king of the dead. Talking about the old king and the new one. Two things in particular it said come floating up in my memory. "Watch the false friend." That one's obvious. I've been wondering about Alex since I heard his voice on the step of the Griffith Observatory.

But what about the wind's other advice? "Beware the dead king." Can Mictlantecuhtli be trusted? Can the wind? What's the angle here? There has to be one. There always is.

"Muerte wants a new king for Mictlan and I fit the bill," I say.

"Don't flatter yourself."

"Then why the hell else do it?"

"She doesn't want a new king" he says. "She wants

the old king back. I was with her for thousands of years. You think she wants some punk to rule by her side? Please. She's going to wait until you're more me than you. Then she's gonna stick a knife between your ribs. The title of Mictlantecuhtli dumps into the best closest candidate. The new king dies and the old one is reborn."

"You come back to life."

"And you're a sacrificial lamb. In theory. We talked about it a long time ago. In case something happened to either one of us. Not like we ever tried it. It might work, it might not. But even if it doesn't pan out, she's still going to kill you."

"I feel special." I knew she wanted to use me for something. Now I know what.

"Hey, that beats the alternative. For both of us. If she doesn't kill you we just keep swapping places. Eventually, you're Mictlantecuhtli and I'm just some schlub."

"Sounds like I get the better end of the deal."

"You think so?" He taps the jade statue's head. "Take a look at me. This is where you're headed. I made this choice. I want this. But you? Eternity's a long time stuck as a rock. I don't care about you. I really don't. But I like it here. I came down here for a reason. My time's over. I want to keep it that way. Your world sucks. I want no part of it."

"The pain in my chest," I say. "Like somebody was ripping out my insides. It's because of that, isn't it? When I use it that's me changing."

"I'm willing to bet you've got some interesting anatomy right about now. A bone or two here, a chunk of a kidney. If a doctor opened you up he'd be scratching his head."

"How come I don't feel any different afterward?"

"Oh, you're fine. Technically. You'll keep on breathing, moving, all that. Until you don't. That pain is part of the process. I said you were being rewritten. I wasn't kidding. You're turning into everything I am. When you use that power and it stops hurting? That's when you should start to worry."

"Say I don't believe you. How do I even know you're telling the truth?"

"You don't. And there's some things I can't tell you. Old agreements. I'd rather you did trust me because we're tied together and it might help me keep you alive and me dead a little bit longer."

"This isn't adding up. If I turn into you how can she even kill me? I'll be a god. What the hell's she gonna shank me with?"

"And realization," he says, "dawning in three . . . two . . . one."

"Oh, sonofabitch. The knife. She's the one who had Sergei steal the knife."

"You're the slow one in your family, aren't you?"

"You're pretty sarcastic for a death god."

"What's funny is that you think I'm speaking English," he says. "I haven't said a word that isn't Nahuatl since I met you. Your brain's doing all the translating. So if I'm coming off as sarcastic, what's that say about you?" I ignore him.

"If she had Sergei get this knife for her, why the hell is he still running around skinning people?" I say.

"It's a guess, but I think she doesn't have him on a very tight leash."

"A guess?"

"It's not like we talk. I made the knife a long time ago for Xipe Totec."

"The farm god."

"Farm god. Please. He's a lot more than that. War, disease, rebirth. He's all over the map. That kind of thing'll make a guy schizophrenic. That knife can do a lot more than just take someone's skin. It can kill damn near anything, including the other gods. When I gave it to him the shit hit the fan and everybody's all freaking out because I gave Mister Bipolar an instrument of mass slaughter. So Huehuecoyotl stole it and got Tlaltecuhtli and Quetzalcoatl to help hide it with some mortals. That Bruja you're hanging out with is from a long line of caretakers."

The rattling off of Aztec names is dizzying. "Out of all of those names I think I caught one," I say. "Quetzalcoatl. Feathered snake god, right?"

He shakes his head. "You better start learning some names quick," he says. "They're family now."

Much as I don't like it I know he's right. The names sound familiar but I haven't had time to dig into all of them. Huehuecoyotl is a trickster, but Tlaltecuhtli is new to me. It took me years to learn all the names of the Voodoo Loa. Most of them are ones you won't find in any books, and I doubt it will take any less time to learn these. Only I don't think I'm going to have years to do it in.

"Okay, so Muerte figures out where the knife is and

sends Sergei after it. But he decides not to give it to her. Goes off the reservation. Why?"

"See these bones?" he says. He kicks at one of the skulls on the floor and his foot sails through it. "These men were led by a priest who couldn't get into his own heaven so he tried to take ours. Hoped to conquer us here the way his people conquered us in your world. From Mictlan he could have moved to any of our other kingdoms."

"Didn't get very far, did he?"

"He got plenty far. But I was able to cut him off from his weapon when I lured him down here. I think Sergei's trying to do the same thing."

"He probably could," I say, thinking of Kettleman. "He's got a guy in his head who probably knows how to do it. But that would take a lot of power, right?" That would explain why he wants the Ebony Cage.

"There's another way," Mictlantecuhtli says. I'm still having a hard time not seeing him as Alex. He doesn't act the way Alex does, not exactly, but he doesn't sound like a millennia-old death god, either. If that's all because of how my mind is translating what he's saying I should probably get my head examined.

"He takes my skin," I say. "I have a connection to this place now, right?"

"Exactly. He also gets your turning into jade problem, so even if he does I doubt he'd last very long."

"You know, this is educational and all, but I got priorities, and whether Sergei gets into Mictlan isn't even on my list. So how is this even my problem? I need

Sergei off my back. Then I can figure out what to do about your crazy ex-wife."

"Or you can use your fucking brain and do both," he says, snapping at me. "You're either deaf or stupid. It's your problem because you need that knife. It can kill gods, jackass. You need to kill her before she kills you and if he gets into Mictlan with it you're never going to see it again."

"No shit. But how the hell am I supposed to find him? If it's a choice between getting dead now or letting him go and getting dead later, I'll take later. I had one way to track him and that's—"

The answer pops into my head. There's only one place he could be right now. He needs the Ebony Cage. It wasn't in the bar. I don't know if Tabitha told him where it is or not, but if she didn't there's only one other person who would know where it is.

"Vivian," I say. "He's at Vivian's. I need to get out of here. I need to get out of here now." A pain like my chest is being torn open by red hot knives hits me as steps carve their way into the wall and up into a new hole in the ceiling. It almost knocks me flat but I catch myself before my knees buckle.

"I wouldn't recommend you keep doing that," Alex says. "It'll just speed things up." He looks up at the hole in the ceiling I just created. "That said, I think you're getting the hang of this. Good luck. That should open up close to where you want to be right now."

The pain fades as I step onto the staircase, not sure if it's going to disintegrate under me if I don't concentrate on it. I made this? It didn't feel like when I cast a spell. It just happened. The stone holds my weight and doesn't disappear underneath me.

"Remember to get that knife," he calls behind me as I run up the stairs. "If she gets it we're both fucked." Right now I don't care about the knife, I don't care about the cage. I'm worried about Vivian.

And that I might be too late.

Chapter 17

Mictlantecuhtli was right. The hole I opened comes up on the sidewalk right in front of Vivian's apartment building on Wilshire. Sergei already had a head start on me before I stepped into Mictlan. No telling if he's already here or not. Without the orb to show me where he is, I'm flying blind.

I run to the building, pop the lock on the front door and go inside. Stairs next to the elevator. I head up to her floor taking steps two at a time. I've got the Browning drawn and a round chambered.

I push through the fire door on her floor and I can tell he's already here. If the crowd of sleepy, panicked neighbors gathered around her door didn't give it away, the sound of the fighting going on inside sure as hell does. I still have the Hi, I'm A COP sticker stuck to my chest and make the best of it, pushing my way through yelling, "LAPD." They barely glance at the blood covering my shirt or register my sunglasses at three a.m.

"That was fast," a gray-haired man in pajamas says. "I just called you guys."

"Rich neighborhood," I say. "What the hell's going on?"

"We started hearing banging a few minutes ago," an Asian woman in a bathrobe says. "I think it's her boyfriend. They started arguing and then we heard that."

"She has a boyfriend?" I say, surprised at my own anger. When the hell did that happen? I mean, okay. Six months since Alex died, I guess that makes sense. But how come I didn't know about it?

"I think so," the woman says, shrinking back from me. "I don't really know."

A tremendous crash comes from the apartment. There's no point knocking and playing the LAPD card. Nobody inside is going to answer. I go to kick the door open and stop when I notice the wards on her door.

Of course she'd have the place warded. If I'm lucky the door just won't break. If I'm not she could have it set to do something nasty instead. Being a doctor and a mage has given her a really ugly edge. I've seen the kind of magic she can do with diseases.

Okay, so how do I get in there? Brute force isn't going to do me much good if I suddenly find myself on the floor puking my guts out and breaking out in boils.

And then, like a kid waving his hand around in class because he thinks he knows the answer, that dark power of Mictlantecuhtli's rears its ugly head. I may not be a god. Not yet. But it seems I've got a god's power.

"I have no idea what you think you can do," I say, "but now's a good time to do it."

Pain flares through my chest. If I wasn't ready for it I'd be on the floor screaming. Even knowing that it's coming doesn't help much. I stagger forward, my vision blurring from the agony. I try to brace myself against the door, but instead I just pass right on through it. I go solid again the second I'm through and the pain subsides, leaving behind an echo of itself that leaves me gasping for air. I wonder what the neighbors are going to think about that?

Vivian's apartment is a mess. Furniture is overturned, books strewn across the floor. Vivian is behind a shield blocking something I can't see that Sergei as Kettleman is throwing at her. His clothes are loose on him, the same ones he was wearing at the bar as the bouncer.

She's wearing a bathrobe and her hair's a mess and I've really missed seeing her and goddamn it why did everything have to go to hell and this really isn't the time to be thinking about that so instead I shoot Sergei.

The bullets get about three inches from him and stop dead, clatter to the floor. I didn't really expect it to work, but I'm still disappointed. At least it distracted him enough that he's stopped his attack.

He turns his attention to me as Vivian lowers her shield. I pop another couple rounds at him. They may not get close but he flinches and in that split second of distraction Vivian hits him with a wall of force that slams him across the room.

Instead of shooting again I run at him. Whatever he's got up keeps me from connecting but his shield is like a suit and it doesn't keep me from wrapping myself around it. I get him in a bear hug, using my momentum to keep moving him across the room. The Kettleman form doesn't have a lot of strength and he can't break out of it.

He could magic his way out, I'm sure, but something that Gabriela said about how the forms the knife gives a person don't actually change the way they think comes to mind. He might be wearing Kettleman's skin and have his abilities, but Sergei's still a brute force kind of guy. At least I hope he is.

He proves me right a second later when he bulks out into the bouncer. He's a little lighter than I remember Sergei being, so it makes sense. Sergei in the bouncer's clothes would be too tight, too restricting. I'm okay with that, because I'm hoping Vivian's paying attention and will help me test a theory.

I let go as soon as he changes forms, letting him throw me off. I hit the ground and roll, getting as far away from him as I can. In this form he's got strength, sure, but he doesn't have any magic. His shield's down. So when Vivian hits him with another blast it blows him straight out through the window of her fourth-story apartment.

He hits the glass hard, shattering it into a thousand shards. He scrambles, trying to grab onto anything. He changes from the bouncer to Sergei to some random guy I've never seen with a black crew cut and porn star mustache. I'm hoping he doesn't change back to Kettleman. With my luck that fucker will probably know how to fly.

I run to the window and watch him fall, flipping

back and forth through bodies and when he hits the ground he's the bouncer. It's a bad fall. Lands on his head and his neck snaps, his limbs whipping around and slapping the pavement below, their bones shattering as they hit. He lies there not moving, twisted into angles human bodies aren't meant for.

Vivian runs to me, breathing hard, wide eyed, questions and accusations written on her face like newspaper headlines. She's about to ask what the hell just happened, what the hell I have to do with it. How, whatever it is, it's got to be my fault. I raise a finger, cutting her off.

"Wait for it," I say.

"Wait for what?"

I'm hoping I'm wrong and that Sergei's as dead as everybody whose skin he's taken, but then the body convulses. Shivers and dances around like it's being pumped full of electricity. Limbs right themselves, his neck snaps back into place. And when it's all back, the skin he's wearing, the poor, dead bastard whose only fault was trying to be a bouncer for a bar in Koreatown, sloughs off like melted wax, leaving a stunned and visibly shaken Sergei in its place.

I pop off a couple rounds from the Browning. I know I won't hit him from this range, but you can't blame a guy for trying. The gunshots shake him out of his stupor and he scrambles to his feet, a look of panic on his face. He bolts down the street.

"Yeah, you run you sonofabitch," I say. I didn't kill him, but now I know something I didn't before. His skins can be killed. And when they do they fall apart.

So he's down one. Too bad he didn't hit the ground as Sergei. Might have saved us all a lot of trouble. Or Sergei might just be another skin at this point.

"What the hell happened?" she says. "Who was that?"

"Are you all right?" I say. I look her up and down. She's got a nasty cut on her cheek and her right temple is bruised.

"I'm fine," she says, pushing my hand away. "What's going on, Eric?"

"His name's Sergei Gusarov," I say. She gives me a blank look. Well, at least I'm not the only person who doesn't know who the hell that is. "He's trying to get the Ebony Cage. He already hit the bar."

"The bar? When? Is anybody hurt?"

"Couple hours ago? I think? My time sense is a little off. Tabitha's in the hospital, she's—Well, she's alive. I made sure she got into an ambulance. It's kind of complicated."

"What hospital?" She picks her way past the debris on the floor, roots around until she finds her cell phone.

"UCLA Westwood," I say. "I think. It got a little weird."

"With you around? Of course it did." She starts punching buttons. "Goddammit. I knew that thing was bad news. I told Alex to get rid of it." She starts shaking, closes her eyes and wills herself to stop. It mostly works, but the adrenaline is still in her system and she can only do so much.

"I thought that was Max," she says. So that was the bouncer's name.

"It sort of was."

She holds up a finger, cutting me off from saying

more as someone answers her call. "Hi, Nancy, this is Doctor Winters." She pauses. "Yeah. I'm calling about a patient who should have been brought in to the ER a little while ago. Korean woman. Tabitha Cheung." Pause. "Yeah, I'll hold. Thanks."

She turns back to me. "What do you mean it was sort of him?"

"It's going to take me longer to explain what the hell is going on than I've got. So short version. The guy we just shoved out the window has a knife that can steal a person's form, memories, everything. It kills them in the process. He got to Max to get to you and Tabitha. Did you tell him where the Ebony Cage is? I know it's not in the bar, anymore."

She stares at me, a dozen questions lighting across her face, decides against all of them. "Yes. It's in a storage unit. I knew there was something wrong when he started talking about the cage. I'd never told him about it and Alex swore he'd never tell any normals about it, either. But I didn't realize that until I'd told him where it was. He doesn't have any of the codes to get inside, though."

Shit. I was hoping he didn't have the location. "And then he changed?"

"Yeah. Into the old guy. Is that Sergei?"

"No," I say. "The guy who walked away from the splat on the sidewalk was Sergei. Old guy was Harvey Kettleman."

"Thought he looked familiar," she says. "Jesus. He used to hang out with my parents—Wait. Does that mean he's dead, too?"

"Few nights ago. Up at Griffith Park. He almost got me, too."

"What does this guy want?"

Telling her what I know would take too long, so I just shrug. "Don't know, but he's already gotten a lot of people killed. And if he's after the cage who knows what he'll do with it."

"A storage place on Santa Monica Boulevard near Cahuenga. Let me write down the entry code." She finds a pen in the mess on the floor and writes some numbers on a business card for a local restaurant. "If you need to get in these codes will do it." She jots down some runes. "And these will deactivate the wards on the unit. You don't want to go in there without doing that first. Whoever triggers it won't live very long. Also, I had to put them up kind of quick. I was going to go back this weekend and do a better job."

"What does that mean?"

"It means if you trigger them there's a decent chance that whatever's inside the unit will get hit, too."

"Oh, Jesus, Viv."

"Fuck you, I was in a hurry. And I didn't think some psycho was going to skin my bouncer and try to kill me for it."

"If these go off will they break the cage?"

"Maybe? How the hell should I know?"

"Does he have this information?"

"No, I didn't give the codes to Max, Sergei—whoever the fuck that was."

"Okay. I shouldn't need to get inside, but he's going to try." I take the card from her and look at the runes.

Some I recognize, others not so much. A combination of ancient languages and hermetic seals, they all combine into a pretty straightforward lock spell, but I can see some things in the patterns that make my skin crawl. "Jesus. Does this one mean 'dysentery'? Whatever happened to do no harm?"

Her eyes go hard. "Hemorrhagic fever. And I tossed that shit out when my boyfriend died."

"Vivian, I—"

"Stop. I know you didn't kill him, but I also know that if it wasn't for you he'd still be alive. So don't even go there." The person on the other end of the phone comes back on and she turns away from me before I can say anything.

"Hi Nancy," she says. "No? Nothing's come in all night?" She gives me a worried glance. "Okay. No, that's fine. Must have the wrong hospital. I'll check with Santa Monica. Thanks." She hangs up the phone.

"They haven't had any ambulances come in since around nine o'clock tonight," she says. "You said Westwood UCLA?"

"Yeah, I—"

I'm interrupted by a banging on the door. "LAPD. Open up."

"Shit," I say. "I kinda told your neighbors I was a cop. Which might not actually cause as many problems as the fact that they saw me phase through the door."

"You got any more of your stickers?" she says.

I pull one out of my pocket along with a Sharpie. "Always," I say, as I uncap the pen and start writing.

"Then make yourself scarce." I'm way ahead of her

and slap a You Can't See Me sticker over the one that says I'm a cop before she's done talking.

"Coming!" she yells and runs to the door. She takes a deep breath, twists her face into one of panic and fear and a second later her eyes tear up. She's a good actress, but I can't imagine it's all that hard right now. She's just been assaulted in her own home. I know she's holding things together well, she always has, but this can't be easy.

She pulls the door open and immediately starts babbling at the two uniformed police. She contradicts herself two, maybe three times. A guy broke in the front door, went out the window. If it isn't for the fact that she's weaving a compulsion spell at the same time she's talking to them I'd be worried for her.

As she leads them further into the living room, I slip past them unseen, hoping I can get to the storage unit before Sergei does.

Chapter 18

I punch in Gabriela's number when I get outside. Sergei's got to know I'm coming and he's not going to be alone. No reason I should be, either. I scan the street for something fast and settle on a Z4 parked nearby. Gabriela picks up as I'm popping the lock and sliding into the driver's seat.

"Tell me this is good news," she says. "I've got a shitstorm going on over here and you're not exactly my favorite person right now."

"Jesus, is anybody ever happy to hear from me? Yes, I've got two bits of good news, as a matter of fact," I say. "If you kill a skin that Sergei's wearing it actually dies. Turns to jellied mush. Really disgusting."

"You killed one of his skins? How?"

"Threw him out a fourth-story window. I was hoping he'd be wearing Kettleman or be himself, but no such luck. The skin sort of ran off him like melted fat.

Also, he definitely can't cast when he's not wearing the Kettleman skin."

"Good to know. Okay, so what's the other good news?"

"I know where he's going. Probably right now, in fact. Storage unit on Santa Monica and Cahuenga, to get that Ebony Cage. If he has anybody left in his crew I'd say it's a good bet he's going to hit it hard. The only plus is that it's warded and he doesn't have the exact unit number, so that'll take him some time."

"Santa Monica and Cahuenga? Hang on." I hear a rustle of paper over the phone. "Okay, I know that place. Any idea why he wants this thing?"

I should probably tell her that I think he's trying to break into Mictlan with it, but I've got an idea forming in my head and the less she knows about what's really going on, the better. I need that knife. Whether Mictlantecuhtli is right about what Santa Muerte is doing or not, if that knife can kill her, I need to get my hands on it. And I really don't think Gabriela's going to be too crazy about that idea.

"No clue," I say.

There's a pause on the phone and I'm not sure she's buying it. "Doesn't really matter, I suppose," she says. "I'm not fucking around this time. I don't care who gets in my way, I'm taking this sonofabitch out. Got me?"

"I'll try to keep my head down," I say. As long as I can get my hands on that knife I don't care what she does. But I really want to kill Sergei. "I'm on my way there now. Meet me a couple blocks away on—Christ, what's down there?"

"Wilcox," she says after a second. "Hey, how's your girlfriend?"

It clicks what Vivian said in her apartment. The ambulance never made it to the hospital. I know it was supposed to go to UCLA Westwood. Would they have sent her to Santa Monica? That's not much further, but it seems unnecessary when Westwood was right down the street. Even after my display of batshit crazy in the ambulance they would have taken care of her.

"I don't know," I say. "She was breathing when I left her."

"That's something," she says. "All right, we'll be there twenty minutes, tops. Don't do anything stupid before we get there."

"Don't worry. I'll wait until you're there before I do anything stupid."

Maybe.

———

It's well past four a.m. and the morning is already gearing up. Delivery trucks and early morning commuters dot the road. The cops have washed away all the drunks and even the hookers on Santa Monica Boulevard have gone in for the night.

I drive past the storage building on the corner of Cahuenga, a twenties Deco building with a clock tower, painted-over windows, and a large parking lot in the back. I doubt they open for another few hours, but the loading doors for the buildings are wide open. The lot's full of cars and about twenty guys standing around like they're waiting for something to happen. This early in the morning it's chilly, but these guys are all wearing long coats too warm for the weather. No doubt to hide their AKs.

It's dark out and the Z4 has tinted glass, but I don't linger too long lest they get ideas and decide to take potshots at me. I don't sense anyone drawing power from the local pool, but that doesn't mean there aren't any mages in that lot. It's not like we wear hats that say "MAGICBOY".

There are a handful of Dead on the streets. Couple murdered tourists, a bum or two. Not enough to cause me problems. I could pop over to the other side, walk right past all of them, and the only guy I'd have to deal with is Kettleman. I don't see him in the parking lot, so he's probably already inside. Pop up behind him and . . . Dammit, I wish I had my straight razor.

Fuck it. I drive around the corner and park out of view of the lot and dial Gabriela. Get her voicemail. "You know how I promised not to do anything stupid until you got here? Yeah, I kinda lied. I'm heading in. Look out for all the guys with AKs in the parking lot. They don't look happy."

I tell myself that this is a smarter approach, anyway. A bunch of people show up and there's going to be bullets and screaming and any chance of surprise we might have is going straight down the toilet. This way I can get in quietly without having to worry about getting shot and get the knife without having to fight Gabriela for it. Because that's really all I care about. Without it, Sergei's useless. If he comes after me, well, he's just a guy wearing a mage suit. I'm a fucking god in training.

And when Gabriela asks me about it, because I know she will, I'll just tell her that I didn't find the knife. He must have hidden it. And if they both happen to survive tonight, they can fight each other over it. With the knife, maybe I can finally get to Santa Muerte and finish this bullshit once and for all.

Once I'm out of the car I check for stray ghosts, extend my senses out to see where the closest ones are. The minute I pop over to the other side I'll have a little while before they start coming for me and not long after that I'll start attracting ones further out. Ten, fifteen minutes and this place is going to be crawling with the Dead. That should give me plenty of time to get into the building and up to the storage unit.

Relying on Mictlantecuhtli's power is too unreliable, and I don't want to do it too often and speed things along. And it fucking hurts. So if I need any more oomph to my magic I may need some blood. I rifle through the Z4's trunk and find a box cutter shoved next to the jack. Perfect.

I wait until I'm close to the lot entrance before I slip over to the other side. The world goes a dull blue-gray and the sounds of the waking street around me disappear into a hollow echo chamber of howling wind. The objects around me glow or slip into shadow depending on how solidly rooted they are in the psychic landscape. The storage building itself glows like it's lit with a blacklight, casting out a sense of solidity. It's been here a long goddamn time. But the cars, streetlights and the car wash across the street all fade away into shadow.

The upshot of all this is that I can walk through the cars, some of the streetlamps and probably even the walls of the car wash, but the storage building is just as solid on this side as it is on the living side. Good thing they left the doors open for me.

I can see Sergei's crew as indistinct blobs of man-shaped light. I can walk through them but it's like stepping into a downpour of cold rainwater. I give them a wide berth and head into the building.

I take a flight of stairs up toward the fourth floor. The elevator won't work for me. I could flip back and press the button, sure, but the minute that car starts moving it'll leave me at the bottom of the shaft. Only the oldest elevators leave enough of a footprint to be solid on this side. I found that out the hard way on the second floor of an apartment building about ten years ago. Damn near broke my neck.

Past the second story I run into a problem. At some point not too long ago they changed out a section of the stairs and moved them in about ten feet. The new stairs are probably substantial enough to hold me, but I'm not entirely sure and they bleed so much into the old ones that I can't tell where the boundary is.

Things get tricky on this side. It's not so much a matter of whether something's been around a long time as it is how much it's been used and what people think about it. Take the Ambassador Hotel. Demolished back in 2005 to make way for a school, but on this side it might as well still be 1968 with Robert Kennedy bleeding out in a kitchen hallway.

Pretty soon the ghosts are going to start converging on this place and hunting me down. And if I flip back to the living side, I'm betting Sergei's left some early warning alarms to tell him if anybody's coming after him. Crap.

I step to the edge of the stairs I know are solid until they blur into the new ones, hope I gauged the distances right and keep going. Everything's fine about five steps up and then my right foot misses the old stairs and disappears into the concrete.

The rest of me follows. It's like stepping into an open manhole cover. My left leg buckles at the knee, slamming into the more solid steps, and I only manage to keep myself from going all the way through by shoving myself against the wall.

Takes a bit, but I manage to swing my right leg up and shimmy up the wall until I can find something solid to put my weight on. This is exactly why I don't like to fly.

Not long and I'm back on the old staircase with only one more floor to go. I'm getting this itch on the back of my mind that's telling me I'm running out of time. I can't see them, but I can feel the ghosts outside coming from all over as they catch whatever passes for my scent in this place. They're close.

It's not like when I summon them and they pop in from all over. Most of them are walking, some of them, the ones that have enough consciousness and intelligence left over from their lives, have figured out that they can just will themselves from place to place. Fortunately, the psychic footprint of the building is going to get in their way just as much as it gets in mine. It'll slow them down, but not by much. And I really don't want to be caught in this stairwell when they come for me.

I step out of the stairwell onto the fourth floor and have to blink to adjust my eyes. The floor has been refitted so many times over the years that most of the walls are some degree of see-through. Plywood has been replaced with plaster and then drywall. The layout of the entire floor has been torn down and rebuilt. Hallways look like rooms look like doorways. It's more confusing than H.H. Holmes' murder hotel.

A wave of dizziness washes over me, but I shake it off. One of the dangers of being on this side too long. It saps your energy, your life, your will. I'm lasting longer than I used to, thanks, I suspect, to my new status as death god in training, but I'm still human enough that it's getting to me. If I don't slide over to the other side soon, I won't have enough energy to do it at all.

I spy a couple of bright lights in the distance. One tall and broad, the other short and slim. Twenty bucks says that's Sergei and his sister. If I'm reading the layout right I might actually be able to make a straight shot for them. There doesn't seem to be anything all that substantial between us. I pop the blade on the box cutter. If I can get close enough to him, I can pop out and take him down before he knows what's hit him. The sister could be a problem, but I might be able to grab the knife before she can react.

I'll have to deal with the ghosts on this side, but if I

can get a wall or two between me and her I can pop back onto the living side and head past most of the ghosts before I have to do it all over again to get past the goons in the parking lot.

Easy.

And that's when the first ghosts come boiling out of the stairwell, howling for my blood.

Chapter 19

A group of ghosts is a fraid. No, really. I don't know what jackass came up with that one, but it's a real thing. A fraid of ghosts. Clearly, they've never seen a group of ghosts. Otherwise it'd be a "Pants-Shitting Terror" of ghosts.

They're like sharks, and near as these ones can tell I'm chum in the water. They feed off life, those little scraps of experience and hope they can barely remember. Guy told me a while ago that as they fade it's because they're draining away to whatever final rest they're going toward, like water circling a drain. I don't know what's on that other side for most of them, but to have your consciousness get stripped away from you like that must be agonizing.

They seethe out of the stairwell like a tsunami, every single one of them wanting a piece of me. One is annoying enough, but twenty will be like running me through a wood chipper. I knew this was going to happen. You hang out on this side for more than a couple of minutes and you will get their attention. I was just hoping I'd already have the drop on Sergei and his sister before they showed.

I have a choice to make. Lose the element of surprise and maybe get killed by the crazy Russian Wonder Twins, or stick around and definitely get killed by the ectoplasmic eating machines. Not much of a choice, really. I concentrate on the spell to flip me back over to the land of the living.

Nothing happens. It's like turning the key in the ignition on a cold morning. I can feel it clicking, but it doesn't turn over.

I don't have time to try it again before they're on me. I turn tail and run. One of the ghosts takes a swipe at me that clips the back of my neck. I feel a flare of icy pain as its fingers connect. I push past the pain and keep running.

With so many tear-downs and rebuilds on this floor it's hard to tell which walls are psychically weak enough to pass through and which are old and solid. There's too much visual clutter. I make a best guess and go down what looks like a collection of store rooms, but over here they could just be old overlapping walls that don't exist anymore.

I'm feeling the effect of the entropy that's sapping my power, but I should be able to pop back over to the other side without a problem. So what the hell is blocking me?

Sergei. With Kettleman's memories he knows who he's up against. Little fucker must have set a trap for me knowing full well that I'd try this trick. Probably has some spell running on this side that's acting like a signal jammer keeping me from crossing back. So where is it and how do I shut it off?

Any wall I can go through the ghosts can go through, too, and they're on my trail like wolves. I need to slow them down, change their focus, if I'm going to have any chance of getting out of this alive. I yank up my sleeve, run the box cutter through the small patch of scarred skin above my left wrist, and shake my arm as I run down the hall.

Blood spatters through the air, droplets landing on the floor behind me. It slows them down as they sense the life scattering around them. A good dozen of the spirits jump on the drops, desperately trying to lap up the blood I'm leaving for them. It won't be enough, though.

I pocket the cutter, pull the Sharpie and some nametags from my pocket. I scribble on them as I run, slapping them on doorjambs, walls, the floor. One wall looks solid and isn't and I almost take a tumble as my hand passes through it. *Draw, O coward. Live not on evil. Sex at noon taxes.* Nonsense palindromes, nothing complicated, but the ghosts jump on them like the good little obsessive-compulsives that they are, stopping to read them backwards and forwards and backwards again. If I had sunflower seeds I'd toss a handful behind for them to stop and count.

Soon I have enough breathing room that I can actually pay attention to what I'm looking for. The blood and palindromes won't hold them long, so I have to work fast. Spells cast over here don't last and I'm cut off from the pool of magic on the living side. So whatever is blocking me has to be actively generating the spell and it has to have enough of its own juice that it can last. Both of those are pretty easy to make.

Now I just need to find the goddamn thing. It could be as small as a ballpoint pen or a scrap of paper. But it should also be pumping out a lot of magic and in this dead place that should be pretty easy to spot. It's harder here because everything gets sucked up by the environment, but I can still feel the magic tugging on the back of my mind the way I can feel it when somebody casts a spell nearby or draws power from the pool.

It takes me almost a minute to find it, mostly because half my attention is on the mass of ghosts all slurping at the drops of blood I left or hovering next to the palindromes in a boiling mass, flowing in and out of each other like water. It's close, which it would have to be. I step slowly through the walls toward it, hoping I don't attract too much attention.

Too late. A few ghosts break off to come snuffling for me like bloodhounds. I bolt, which gets some of the others' attention. I need to find this thing fast. The tugging in the back of my head gets stronger in one direction, weaker in another. I'm playing a game of hot and cold with a swarm of ghosts on my heels.

And then I see it. A cell phone on the floor. I grab it, see runes on the back written in crayon, of all things. I wipe them away with my thumb and that pressure I've been feeling in the back of my mind cuts off as the spell breaks. That it was written in crayon is weird, but I don't have time to think about it. The rest of the ghosts are almost on me.

I flip back to the land of the living. Color and sound all rush at me as the world solidifies. I find myself inside one of the storage units as the nearest ghost takes a swipe for me. The ghosts and I can still see each other, but now they can't touch me. Frustrated, they swarm around and through me, claw at a meal they can't get to anymore. I stick out my tongue and give them the finger.

The cellphone I brought back with me from the other side buzzes in my hand. I look at it, confused, then see a coffee can on the floor with a Bluetooth headset taped to it, wires sticking out and ending in a brick of white plasticine stuck to the top. Good bet that's not coffee in there.

I'm in a locked storage unit with a bomb about to go off and surrounded by ghosts who want to eat me. Nicely done, Sergei, you clever sonofabitch. I didn't just walk, I fucking ran into this trap.

This is gonna suck.

I turn toward the wall, break into a run. I've only got about five or six feet of space, but if I time it right I might survive. I run through the ghosts and then, just as I'm about to hit the wall, I flip over to the dead side.

And the bomb goes off. I transition before the shock wave hits. I watch the room disintegrate in silence around me. I run through the ghosts as they realize their meal's back on the table. Hands and teeth rake through my skin, a hundred razor-sharp soldering irons. I keep moving, push past the pain, shove my way through the crowd until I'm a good four or five hallways past the unit that just blew up. Shift back before the ghosts can take anything else off of me.

Light and smoke and sound crash in on me and I collapse to the floor in the middle of a hallway. Fire alarms going off, water spraying from overhead sprinklers. My arms and back where the ghosts hit me feel like they're on fire. My right hand is crossed with welts, each line glowing faintly like white fire under the skin. I try to make a fist, but even moving it is agony.

I drag myself from the floor. A wave of nausea hits me and I throw up. The ghosts are still swarming around me, harmless on this side. Probably more confused than ever. I swat at a few of them, my hand passing harmlessly through cold spots. They don't care. They still think they're getting a free meal.

On the other side it was hard to really get a sense of the current layout. Too many confusing walls from the past overlapping one another. But on this side there are signs and numbered doors. Even through the smoke I can tell where I am. From where I saw Sergei and his sister it's clear they still don't know where the Ebony Cage is. Vivian's unit is on the other side of the building from where I saw them. Just around the corner from me.

I laugh, wiping my mouth with my sleeve. "They're digging in the wrong place." I lean against the wall, glad to feel something solid. That's not the longest time I've spent on the other side, but it's damn close and the first time I've been hit by that many ghosts. Everything hurts. The spots where they tagged me feel like they're on fire. I'm feeling drained and weak. With the amount of magic I expended and that the other side drained from me I doubt I've got enough left to light a fart. But I'm going to have to move. The only advantage I might have is if Sergei thinks I'm dead. And if I tap the local pool to fill up, he's going to know I'm not.

I don't sense any new magic going off, but that doesn't mean much. Gotta hand it to him, he's smarter than I thought. Get me stuck on the other side, give me the way to get out, and the minute I use it, set a bomb off under my feet. Well played. I'm going to enjoy killing him.

With Kettleman's skill Sergei could have set some more warning triggers and I might not know it, but I'm hoping he was expecting the bomb to take care of that for him. If he's betting on the Ebony Cage to get him into Mictlan then he doesn't need me anymore. I'm just a loose end that needs tying up.

Gunfire erupts in the distance, cutting through the sounds of the fire alarm. Hard to tell but I don't think it's inside the building. That won't last. A second later my phone buzzes in my pocket and I almost have a heart attack thinking it's Sergei's detonator. I pull it out to see the number. Gabriela. Looks like she's called me a couple times already. No coverage in the lands of the dead.

I answer the phone. "So glad I'm not trying to sneak up on the bad guy or anything," I say.

"Then turn off your goddamn ringer. If you're where I think you are you already blew your cover," Gabriela says. "You're going to get yourself killed."

"One of these days, probably. And how's your evening going?"

"Was that explosion you?" she says.

"Are those gunshots you?" I say back.

"You sound delirious," she says. Pause for more gunfire. "You hurt?"

"Ghosts tried to eat me. Sergei tried to blow me up. I've been better."

"What floor are you on?"

"Fourth. Come on up, we'll have some laughs. Sergei and his sister are around here, somewhere. Maybe we can double date. Get milk shakes, hit the sock hop later."

"Jesus, you are in bad shape. What the hell were you thinking?"

"Seemed like a good idea at the time?"

"You are such a pain in the ass," she says.

"Part of my charm."

"Sure, keep telling yourself that."

The wall in front of me shimmers, glows blue. I'm too slow and before I can react Sergei, wearing his original-issue Russian mobster body, steps out of the wall with a big-ass Desert Eagle in his hand.

And he shoots me.

Chapter 20

The magic in my tats does what it can to protect me and there's a blinding flash of light and heat as the spells bleed off the energy of the round before it hits me. But a big fucking bullet's a big fucking bullet and it blows a hole right through my abdomen. It's so fast and so intense it takes me a second to register what's happened. My legs drop out from under me, the phone falls from my hand.

Sergei's sister steps through the wall behind him. Her steps tentative, eyes wide, like she's not sure what's happening. She peeks around his shoulder like a spooked pet and it occurs to me that maybe she doesn't really know what's happening. Compared to him, she's tiny. Maybe five foot six, but folded in on herself, dwarfed not only by Sergei's size, but by his personality, too. On the train she came across as crazed. Living in the shadow of a brother like that, I can see why.

"Bro," Sergei says, leaning down and getting into my face. It's hard to hear him past the ringing in my ears. It occurs to me that this is the first time I've actually heard him speak. Where Kettleman's voice is clear and crisp, Sergei speaks English as a second language, his Russian accent thick like cold molasses. A smile splits his face like a crack in the earth, showing three gold teeth on the left side. He's wearing a baggy t-shirt and sweatpants. Probably got tired of his body shrinking and growing and his clothes not keeping up. I press a hand against my belly to keep my guts in place. The initial shock is starting to wear off and the pain is kicking in.

"Sergei, buddy," I say through gritted teeth. "Been looking for ya."

"And here I am," he says. "Glad you didn't die, bro. Still want your skin."

"You probably shouldn't have put a hole in it, then."

He laughs. "I fix that as soon as I take it."

"You take it? I thought your little sister was gonna get it. She almost got me on the train."

His brow furrows, face twisting into a frown that looks like a rockslide. He turns to her. "This true?"

"What, you didn't know?" I say. "Oh, man, it was epic. She killed, what, twenty, thirty people on that train? More? How'd you get away, anyway?"

"What is this?" he says. "What is this about a train?"

She shrinks away from him like he's on fire. "I saw him. When I was by the bar. Just as you described him. And the knife was in the car. So I followed him. He took the train and I followed him." She lifts herself to her full height and it's like watching an angry flower defying the sun.

He slaps her with the back of his hand, a bone-jarring crack that echoes in the hallway. She shrinks back into herself, but it only lasts a moment before she's back in his face again, an angry bruise blooming on her face.

"You promised me," Katya screams. "You promised me a skin."

"When I am done. Not before. I told you this."

"When you're done. Always when you're done. When will that be? You have had weeks and only now you move."

"Soon I will have the cage and I will finish this. So shut up and let me do that." They start screaming at each other in Russian. I have no idea what they're saying, but it can't be good.

I'm losing a lot of blood, feeling kind of woozy and goddamn this hurts. And that's probably why it's taken me this long to realize Sergei's Sergei. He's not wearing Kettleman.

He can't cast spells.

I don't have a lot of power left, but I have enough. I push past the pain, focus my will and send out a blast of lightning that fills the hallway. The blast hits them both, but Sergei's fast. The moment my spell goes off he's Kettleman again, throwing up a shield that protects him from the worst of it. It shoves him hard against the wall, but it doesn't take him down. Katya, on the other hand, gets the brunt of it. She hits the floor, spasms with the voltage.

Sergei throws out a spell of his own and my throat squeezes closed as the air tightens around my neck. He lifts me up, my feet dangling inches off the floor. I can't breathe, I'm bleeding out and my head feels like it's about to pop off my neck. My vision is starting to go dark around the edges. I'm not sure what's going to kill me faster, blood loss or asphyxiation.

"That was very foolish, Mister Carter," Sergei says in the crisp, clipped tones of Kettleman's scholarly voice. He looks over at his sister lying on the ground. She's stopped convulsing, but I doubt she's dead. The pressure around my throat loosens and I can breathe again. I suck in air with a loud wheeze.

"I was hoping I could just take your skin without a fuss," he says. "Not that I need it, anymore. Maybe I should just kill you. What do you think?"

"How are you gonna get into Mictlan without it? That is your plan, right? Use my connection to Santa Muerte to get there? She been whispering in your ear, telling you what to do, and you just got sick of it? That about the size of things?"

"Nicely done," he says. "Her, or someone like her. I don't like being made a puppet."

"More the puppet master type?"

"Quite. That was the plan, yes. But if I take your skin, it's not really my power, is it? It's like wearing a suit of clothes. That's all these are. Costumes. They're not really me. But imagine if I can kill a god. I could take all of Mictlan."

"You're an idiot. You ever wonder why Kettleman didn't try something like that already?"

"Because he was weak," he says.

"Because he wasn't stupid. Yeah, you might know what he knew, but it hasn't made you any smarter. It's just made you more confused. You're like a monkey with an education."

"I wouldn't expect you to understand," he says. "You've already thrown away the gifts Santa Muerte's given you. I don't think I want your tainted point of view in my head. And once I have the Ebony Cage I'll have more than enough power to punch through to Mictlan. I don't need you at all."

"Gotta keep me around a little longer, at least," I say.

"Oh? Why's that?"

"Storage unit's locked." I'm starting to slur. "Warded. You might be able to break in, but you'll destroy the cage if you do."

"I see. I suppose you have the key, then?"

"Right here in my pock—Goddammit. Can we go back to before I told you where the key is?"

"Blood loss is not your friend, Mister Carter. Kindly hand me the key." He steps close, puts his hand out. I reach into my pocket. Of course I don't have a key. But I do have this exploding marble that Gabriela gave me at her hotel.

I pull it out and shove it into his eye.

He screams as his eyeball pops with a squelch, my thumb digging into the socket and cramming the marble in as hard as I can. Gabriela said it would only effect the space of whatever it was used in, from a suitcase to a whole room. I wonder what it'll do to the inside of his skull.

I pull my thumb out of his eye and he falls back, the spell holding me up dissipating as he claws at his face. I drop to the floor. He flails, tries to dig out the marble. I trigger it with a thought.

Sergei's face lights up from the inside. His screams are drowned by the jet engine sound of the fire and smoke flaring out of his eyeballs, nose, ears and mouth, charring and blistering his skin. He convulses, falls to his knees. The light dies and then, a beat later, the implosion hits. Air pulls in through every hole in his head, the skull cracking under the pressure. He falls face-first to the floor. His head disintegrates into powder.

That little bauble might have killed the Kettleman skin, but I doubt it took out Sergei. I don't have much time before he comes back. I crawl over to him, grab his gun. Rifle through his pockets until I find the obsidian knife, slip it into my coat pocket. Then I plant myself a few feet away against the wall, the gun heavy in my hand and wait for him to come back.

I don't know if he could have broken through to Mictlan or not. With Kettleman's skill and the Ebony Cage, I'd say that's a definite maybe. But now he's just a Russian mobster and the second he moves he'll be a dead Russian mobster. And if he throws another skin at me, well, this gun holds a lot of bullets.

"You killed him," Katya says, her voice barely above a whisper. She lifts her head, smoke curling up from her hair.

"Nah, he ain't dead," I say. "Gonna be. But he isn't, yet. And don't you get any ideas."

"Are you going to kill me?"

Good question. "Probably. I mean you did kill a lot of people."

"I didn't know what would happen to those people on the train," she says. "It's not my fault."

"I'm sure Mrs. O'Leary's cow felt the same way."

"Who?"

"Never mind. You know what? Go. You don't deserve to get away, but I'm feeling kind of woozy and I'm tired of dealing with you. I see you again and I will kill you."

"Don't I get a vote?" Gabriela rounds the corner, machete held loose in her hand. Face is covered in soot, cut on her cheek that'll need stitches, left eye going black from a nasty hit. "Jesus, Carter you look like shit."

"Blame him," I say. The pain in my stomach is like somebody punched me with a burning coal. Vision's getting worse. It occurs to me that I might actually die here. Huh.

"Sergei?"

"Yeah. Might not want to get too close. He was Kettleman when I burned him. He's gonna get all goopy in a second and then I'm gonna shoot him."

"The hell did you do to him?"

"Those little marble bombs of yours work a treat." Sergei's body shudders, the skin rippling like a pool after a stone's been thrown in. It turns waxy, translucent and then gushes off of him like a popped water balloon. And there's Sergei, lying in a puddle of thick, pink sludge, a bewildered look on his face.

Blood loss will really screw with your reflexes. It takes a moment before I register that Sergei's back and for my brain to tell my finger to pull the trigger. And in that brief second Katya tosses out another of those goddamn paper charms her brother made for her.

The rolled up wad of paper hits the floor between Sergei and I and flares like flash paper. Cracks split the concrete floor, the drywall, the acoustic tile ceiling. Massive branches of ice explode out of the cracks, a razor sharp lattice that blocks my view as I pull the trigger. The Desert Eagle bucks with so much force that it flies out of my hand and carves a divot in the drywall behind me. The bullet hits the translucent wall of ice, cascading a web of cracks through its surface, but stops dead.

Gabriela grabs me and yanks me hard out of the way as more shards extend through the floor. One of them slices my leg, but I barely feel it. I'm pretty much numb from the stomach down. By the time the ice is done it's a solid wall of interlocking spears five feet deep blocking the entire hallway. Maybe three seconds have gone by.

Gabriela is yelling at me, but I can't hear her over the ringing in my ears. She gets under my arm and hauls me to my feet and I think I'm screaming and everything goes black for a second and then I'm being dragged down the other end of the hall. The ringing starts to fade and I can kind of make out her asking me where the Ebony Cage is.

"Hang on," I say, and I know I'm yelling and I'm starting to notice the pain in my right hand. I think I broke it when I fired that goddamn gun. Who the hell invents a gun that can break your fucking hand just by shooting it? I scan the numbers on the storage units, blinking a couple times before they get right in my vision.

"Next right and one down." She nods and we get back to dragging my sorry ass down the hall.

She asks me something and I yell "What?"

"You gonna make it?" she says. I think.

"I don't know," I say, though I have to admit to myself that it's really more "probably not." I shift my left hand a little because I can feel something thick and slimy squirm around the hole in my gut and I think it might be my intestines.

"I thought you had protection. Your tats."

"You make it sound like I forgot condoms. Cut me some slack. I should be a smear on the fucking wall."

"Police and fire's gonna be here soon if they're not already," she says.

"Then we'd better hurry. If Sergei gets the cage it could get ugly." Gabriela helps me stand. My left leg is limp and dragging behind me and every move is agony, but at least I'm upright.

"Not like he could do anything with it. You killed Kettleman, right?"

"I don't know how much he's going to remember now that he doesn't have Kettleman to fall back on, but if he knows enough to remember what it is I wouldn't put it past him to try. It's not easy, but it's like a toddler with a hand grenade."

"I don't care if he blows up the whole goddamn block. I just want to get the knife back."

"Yeah. We'll get it back." I should probably tell her

I've got it in my pocket, but if I manage to live through this I'm going to need it. And if I don't, well, I won't care then, will I?

"And kill him," she says.

"Figured that was a given."

We round the corner. I see Sergei down the hall sitting on the floor, head in his hands. Weeping. Seriously, he's crying like somebody just shot his dog. Big, wracking sobs.

"I've heard of this," Gabriela says. "After a while the skins become a part of you. Pretty traumatic when they go. Lose a big part of yourself. Kinda tragic when you think about it."

"We're still gonna kill him, right?"

"Oh, fuck yes."

Katya is fiddling with the padlock, yanking on it, hitting it with her hands. It's not budging. She sees us at the end of the hallway, digs something out of her pocket. Another one of those goddamn paper charms? How many of those things does she have?

"You really don't want to do that," I yell.

"Don't come any closer!" she screams. She looks crazier than on the train. "I'll do it. And it—" She looks at the wadded up paper in her hand. "It will kill you."

"You have no idea what that one does, do you? You honestly think it won't fuck you up, too? Come on. Give it up and we'll let you go."

"The fuck we will," Gabriela says and throws her machete. It zips through the air, helped along, no doubt with whatever charms she's spelled into its blade. The second it leaves her hand, Katya tosses the paper charm. It's a toss-up which hits first, the paper to the floor or the machete three inches deep through Katya's skull. When the paper hits there's that telltale flash, but instead of ice or a life-sucking wave of energy, nothing happens.

For about two seconds. Then the earthquake hits.

The whole building wrenches to one side. Cracks tear through the walls, the ceiling crumbles. A heavy shock bounces me off the wall as it throws Gabriela across the hallway. Huge cracks rip through the building, disintegrating the concrete beneath our feet. The floor opens up beneath me.

And I fall.

Chapter 21

I come to in a pile of shattered concrete, blink dust out of my eyes. Flickering light from busted fluorescents cast strobe shadows across the rubble. I can't feel anything below my chest, which is probably a good thing, because I've got a two-foot length of rebar sticking through my left leg.

"Carter?" Gabriela says. It's a supreme effort of will, but I finally twist my head around to look for her.

"I'm here," I say. "You know, I really wish you hadn't split her head open like a fuckin' pumpkin up there."

"You said you weren't gonna kill her," she says, closer, but I still can't see her.

"Yeah. That's what you say to a person when you don't want them to set off a big goddamn spell. Not kill her. Jesus. What am I, an idiot? Of course I was gonna kill her. And who the fuck sets off an earthquake in Los Angeles? That's just rude." I cough, a thick, wet sound that ends in me spitting blood. That's probably not good.

Gabriela crawls over a pile of rubble toward me. "Oh, shit."

"What? My hair messed up?" The joke falls flat and she stares at me like she's looking at new roadkill.

"You're really fucked up, man. Can you move?"

I get my arms up underneath me and push myself to sitting. The pain from the gunshot is mostly pressure and though I can move my legs with a lot of difficulty, I can't feel them. I don't want to think about what that means.

"Sort of? How far did we fall?"

"Three? Four floors? I think we're on the ground," she says.

There's a rumble nearby as debris shifts. Sergei and Katya pull themselves from the wreckage, their forms shifting in the flickering light. Sergei's head and body are overflowing with bulbous tumors, blood and pus running from multiple ruptures in his skin. Katya has the machete firmly embedded in her skull. Neither of them seem particularly bothered by this.

"I think they broke the cage," Gabriela says.

"What was your first clue?" The earthquake must have cracked the door, setting off the wards Vivian put on it. That would explain the tumors covering Sergei's body.

Katya grasps the handle of the machete with both hands and wrenches it out of her forehead. Thick blood wells up from the wound and dribbles down her face. She flings the machete to the side with enough force to embed it into a concrete support.

"And they're dead?" Gabriela says.

"I'm going with yes." Sergei probably died of terminal cancer in seconds. And when the cage broke open, the demons trapped inside would have gotten out. With their bodies twisted into the frame of the cage they'd need new ones. Nice of Sergei and Katya to leave a couple lying around for them.

"We need to leave," I say. I don't know about Gabriela but between all the power I've used up just getting to this point and the fact that I can barely think straight from blood loss, I'm tapped. I can just make out the remains of a still-glowing exit sign behind us. I start to half limp, half drag my useless legs over the rubble toward it.

There's a flash in my peripheral vision, a sudden blur of motion that spins by and then Katya's in front of me, her face covered in rivulets of draining blood. She knocks me to the ground with a fist as hard as iron, slams Gabriela in the throat with an open palm, dropping her before she can get a spell off.

I try to stand, but I don't get very far before Sergei grabs me by the throat and lifts me in the air. The eyes peeking through that mass of tumors are dead. Like all those skins he was taking, he's become a suit of clothing for something else. I slap at him but there's no strength in it. I pull in power from the local pool, but it's too little, too late.

Gabriela lets loose from the ground with a gust of wind that blows Katya a good twenty feet across the remains of the room. She hits the wall hard, shakes it off like a dog shaking off water. Another blur of motion and Gabriela's against a support beam, the demon's hand white-knuckled around her throat.

My thoughts slide off each other like Teflon. I try to think of something, anything that can help. If Gabriela dies I'm one step behind her. Hell, I might be in front of her with how fucked up I am. If these demons don't take me out, my injuries will. It would be really easy to just slip into nothing. To fade away and stop having to worry about demons and magic knives and death gods. It's enticing. I like the idea. What the hell am I going to do anyway? There's no way in hell I'm walking out of this building. So fuck it, I give up. Stick a fork in me, folks. I'm done.

But then that dark power hiding in my bones decides now's a good time to remind me that it's not necessarily my choice.

It flares inside me, spreading like cold fire through my veins, muscles, mind. Before there was pain, burning, a wrenching like I was being torn apart. This time it's just the feeling of raw power flooding through me. I know this is a bad sign, but right now I've got more important things to take care of. The hole in my gut closes over, bones knit, organs and blood vessels seal. Each healed injury leaves a cold gap, not quite numb, not quite alive. All my wounds fill up with something that isn't me.

I pull the rebar out of my thigh, shove it hard up through Sergei's tumor-ridden throat. Blood and green pus ooze out of the wound. It doesn't slow him down, of course. He's already dead, but it's pretty satisfying. I still can't breathe from Sergei's hand around my throat and I don't know if he can kill me. Safer to assume that he can.

The last time I used this power I didn't know what to do. I still don't, not really, but I do know one trick. I grab his hand. The moment I touch him he starts to disintegrate like sand being washed away by the tide. He recoils, confusion and pain showing through those dead eyes. Flaps his arm, slaps at it to make it stop, but it doesn't help. I leave him trying to put out a fire that isn't there.

When I turn back to Gabriela she's gotten out of Katya's grip and is swinging a busted 2x4 at her. Katya yanks it out of her hand before it can connect. Seems that might have been the plan. Gabriela jumps back, snaps her fingers and the wood bursts into flame, spreading quickly up Katya's arms. The room fills with the smell of burning hair and meat.

The grin on Gabriela's face disappears just as quickly when she realizes the fire doesn't seem to be bothering her. Katya throws the burning 2x4 aside and, fully engulfed in flames, takes a swing. Gabriela ducks under the fist, but gets a knee in her face for her trouble. I grab a hunk of concrete the size of a softball and lob it at Katya's head. It hits hard enough to knock her over. Gabriela takes the hint, scrambles past her to the exit.

Katya sits on the floor, fire crawling over her skin, blackening it like barbecued chicken. Laughing. "I saw what you did," she says. "It won't help."

"Oh, I don't know. Worked great on him."

"But can you destroy the rest of us?" A rising whisper grows behind me. I chance a glance over my shoulder. Shadows rising up out of the rubble like wisps of smoke. "Hundreds of us in that cage, wizard. Trapped for ten thousand years. Some of us will find bodies from the dead, but some of us are choosier." She sniffs at the air like a bloodhound. "And I smell so many living right on the other side of that door."

Gabriela's crew, Sergei's men, the police and firemen who have no doubt surrounded the place wondering what in the hell is going on in here. If those demons get out we're all fucked. Even if I run around the room doing my destructo thing there is no way I'm going to hit them all, and even with Mictlantecuhtli's power running through my veins it doesn't mean they can't kill me, or worse, possess me.

They need to be put back into a prison, and I think I know someplace that'll fit the bill nicely. I don't know how I do it the same way that I don't know how I bend my leg, blink my eye, but I know it can be done, because I watched Mictlantecuhtli do it a few hours ago.

With a thought a hole tears open in the floor, belching out a smell of dry desert, desiccated rot. A powerful wind builds up around it, pulling up dirt, debris, concrete and rebar. The contents of the storage units, bicycles, furniture, scattered books, the random detritus of people's lives, are swept up in that hurricane. Katya grabs hold of a jutting beam as the floor disappears beneath her, but the wind grabs her and yanks her down into the hole.

The pit extends around me, sucking everything in. I can see the shadowy forms of the freed demons trying to find some purchase, some surface to root to. A deafening roar fills the room as the wind pulls them down like water in a drain. I make sure every last one of them is shoved down that hole and then I close it up behind them with a thundering crash.

And then it ends. Silence. Nothing but Gabriela and I standing in an empty, bombed out room, scoured clean. "What did you do to them?" she says.

"Sent them all to Mictlan." I think. Possibly just to Mictlantecuhtli's tomb. Man, will he be pissed. I wonder if maybe I should have tossed a match down the hole, too. Start a fire to make the Santa Anas happy.

"And the knife?"

I pull it out of my coat pocket, show it to her. "I can't give it back," I say. "Not yet. That gonna be a problem?"

"Something tells me you've got a bigger claim to that thing right now than I do."

"Thanks." I slide it back into my pocket. "You want to get out of here?"

"I would love to."

———

Getting past the cops turns out to be the easy part. The quake destroyed most of the building we were in and the shockwave nearly leveled the surrounding blocks. When we get out of the building most everyone's been called away to deal with the fallout. There's hardly anyone in the parking lot. A couple of don't-look-at-me spells get us onto the street pretty quickly.

Santa Monica Boulevard is a mess of downed lines and burst pipes flooding the streets. Cars are flipped, power's out. Dawn has lit the east with pink, but it's still strange not to see the streetlights.

"I was gonna suggest we take my car," I say, "but there doesn't seem to be a street to drive it on."

"I can walk if you can," she says. "You can, right? You're not gonna keel over now that everything's over?"

I pull up my blood-covered shirt and look at the space where the bullet tore through. There's no scarring, but the new skin is a deep green. I roll up my sleeve to look at the furrows where the ghosts tagged me. Same thing. The skin moves as I move, bending and shifting when I breathe. But when I touch it, it's cold and hard. I tap it with a fingernail. It sounds like glass.

"What is that?"

"Jade," I say.

"Do I want to know?"

"It's a long story." Fuck. I hadn't wanted to believe Mictlantecuhtli, but it seems he's right. I'm beginning to become him. His power, his condition. I have no idea how long it will be before I end up a jade statue sitting in some corner basement of Mictlan.

"We're gonna be walking a while," she says. "Think we got time for a long story." Fair point. So I tell her. We walk for a long time, picking our way past the worst of the quake damage; holes in the pavement, cockeyed buildings on cracked foundations. News helicopters overhead are surveying the damage. Earthquakes are old hat for Angelenos, and though we see a few dozen skittish people waiting for the aftershocks, most are staying indoors, provided their buildings are still standing.

By the time I'm done talking we're coming up on Sunset Boulevard. The damage isn't as bad here. Signal lights have power, no downed lines. The flooding is limited to a couple of busted hydrants.

"And you're sure this is going to happen to you?" Gabriela says. "That you'll swap places with him?"

"No," I say. "I trust him as far as I can spit a rat. But he's been right about the jade. He's right that I've got his power, even though it seems to have its own idea of when to show up."

"Can you still do that thing? The hole to Mictlan?"

"Don't know. I think it's gone again. I feel . . . different when it's happening, though this last time at least it didn't hurt." I remember him saying that was a bad sign.

"Well, good luck." She stops at a Tercel that's covered in a layer of concrete dust. "You want a ride or you want to find your own?"

"I'm good." After dumping out everything that's happened I'd rather spend some time alone to think about it.

"Okay." She slides into the driver's seat, starts the car with a touch of a finger. "Just one thing. And I think it's something you should think about. Because it might change how you do things, how you look at things. I'm not saying that what's happening to you is good or bad. I think it's fucked up, but we both know that there's shit out there that's bigger than either one of us and sometimes we don't get to pick the part we play in it."

"You asking if I'm all right with this?"

"No. I'm asking if you're still you. If you're really swapping places with this guy, how sure are you that the choices you're making are yours and not his?"

The question stops me. I thought I knew what I was when I left L.A. fifteen years ago, some punk kid trying to make things better, and that was wrong. And then I came back thinking I knew what I was, some cold professional who didn't let his personal life get in the way, and that turned out to be wrong, too.

And now. Now I have no idea what I am.

"If I find an answer, I'll let you know."

She laughs. "I'd kinda rather you didn't. No offense, Eric, but I've got enough trouble without you showing up again. I have a lot of pieces to pick up, a lot of people to find and probably get out of jail. Something tells me you're better at breaking things apart than you are at putting them back together again."

"Seems that way sometimes. Take care of yourself."

"You too." I watch her drive off, the sun peeking over the horizon, and worry that she's right.

Chapter 22

I steal a Volvo parked in front of a Thai restaurant and make my way back to my motel in Burbank. The freeway's closed, either from actual damage or the fear of it, so I cut up through Glendale. An eerie calm has settled over the streets. Reminds me of the Northridge Quake in '94. Not as big, not by a longshot, but it's got people spooked. Quakes have aftershocks, but since this wasn't a real quake, there won't be one. The tension of waiting for the next shoe to drop hangs heavy in the air.

I turn on the radio, tune past the AM Spanish stations and get some news in English. Quake's the big story, but so is the storage facility. They're calling it gang warfare. Big firefight. I listen for a while and then the train story comes on. Media's chewing on a terrorism angle, but the official story is a gas leak in the train car. It's amazing the stories people come up with to explain the shit they can't explain. And then there's a brushfire out in Lancaster. Blame's on a sudden Santa Ana wind that's kicked up overnight and an errant spark. It's a weird feeling, being responsible for so much of the news.

I pull into the parking lot of the motel, kill the engine and sit there, fried. I want to take a blistering-hot shower, sleep for a week, burn these clothes. I don't think I've ever bled so much in my life. I touch the spot where the bullet went in, feel the cool texture of the stone that's replaced the flesh. I take a breath and it moves with me, but there's a stiffness to it that's going to take some getting used to. I just hope I don't have to get used to any more of it.

My phone rings in my pocket. I answer as soon as I see that it's Vivian. "Hey. How's Tabitha?" I say.

"I don't know," she says. She sounds exhausted. "I've called every emergency room in L.A., I've called the police. No one's seen her. Nobody's seen that ambulance."

"It had to go somewhere," I say. "After the shit I pulled I'm surprised they didn't go straight to the cops."

"These things have GPS installed. They don't just disappear. It should have turned up by now. Do you think the guy who was going after the cage—"

"It's not him. He's dead. And I don't think he had time to do anything to her. You've tried her phone?" I say.

"Home, cell, the bar. Nothing."

"She's probably fine and this is just confusion from the quake. She'll turn up."

"I know, but even with all that it's weird. I'm going on shift in a little bit and I can't keep tracking her down."

"I got it from here," I say. "I'll find her."

"Thanks. Let me know if you hear anything."

"I'll keep you posted." I disconnect, wondering what the hell could have happened. A thought pops into my head, something Mictlantecuhtli said about his connection to me. I push it out of my mind, but it comes back stronger along with a question I hadn't asked before. The more I think about it, the less I like it.

Goddammit. I just want to go to sleep, but this just gets bigger and bigger in my mind and I can't shake it. Finally I resign myself to it. There's nothing I can do about it until I get a shower and some clean clothes, but a nap is out of the question. I head inside past the motel ghosts and hope I'm wrong.

———

I pull up outside Tabitha's house. I button the topmost button on my shirt, straighten my tie. Now, not only do my tattoos peek up over the collar, but thin green streaks do, as well. All of the wounds from where the ghosts tagged me have filled in with jade, and now green lines crisscross my body underneath the tats. I don't know how many of the tattoos are still useful, or if there's even any way I can touch them up. Maybe with a dremel? I cut myself at the motel to see if I could score the jade. Couldn't even scratch it. But cutting actual flesh is fine. I was half worried it would heal over with more jade, but it bled like any other cut.

I sit in the car for a good five minutes drumming my fingers on the steering wheel. Thought a lot on the drive over. Didn't like what I came up with. Eventually it's shit-or-get-off-the-pot time and I finally get out of the car. The blooming jacaranda tree in Tabitha's front yard is an explosion of purple. Petals litter the ground in a violet blanket. I pause a moment to look at the Mini. It was in the bar lot last night. There's no way any self-respecting hospital would have let her leave so soon. So did someone else drive it here? Who? Someone from the bar? Some old friend she calls when things get tough? It occurs to me that Tabitha knows a lot more about me than I know about her. I go to the front door, not sure I want to go inside, not sure I want to stay out here. There are answers on the other side of that door that I'm not sure I want. I'm afraid that there might be more questions, too. We have precious few illusions and I'm afraid that a big one is about to get broken. I take a deep breath, try the knob. Unlocked.

Nothing's changed inside, boxes in varying stages of unpacking, pictures leaning against the wall rather than hung up, but there are things I didn't notice before. Last night I wasn't paying as much attention to my surroundings as I should have. Too focused on being beat to hell, my own problems, on Tabitha. Now that I get a good look around in the daylight, I can see the little things. Small details that didn't register. A skeletal marionette carved of wood hanging from a hook in the corner, a line of ceramic *calaveras* on the mantel painted in bright Dia De Los Muertos patterns.

Tabitha steps out from her kitchen, two mugs of coffee in her hands. "Black, right? I've never asked, but you always struck me as someone who drinks his coffee black." She tries to hand a mug to me. I don't take it. She shrugs and sets it on the coffee table.

"Vivian's been calling," I say. "Trying to find out what happened to you. You haven't answered your phone."

"Of course I haven't answered the phone. I don't want to talk to her. I want to talk to you."

"Tell me I'm wrong," I say. "Tell me you didn't lie to me. That you saw Alex and he told you where I was and that I'm wrong."

She sips at her coffee. "I can't," she says. "And you know that." I do. I wish I didn't. Wish this was all a mistake and I was just making shit up in my head. But I knew the truth before I got here. Knew it before I was even conscious of it, I think.

"How long have you been Santa Muerte's puppet? Were you working with her the whole time I've known you?" When Mictlantecuhtli told me about his connection to me, something bothered me, but I couldn't place what. And then things happened so fast I didn't have time to think about it after. But after talking to Vivian it started to bug me again. And that's when it clicked. How she found me at the store, how Santa Muerte told me in the desert that I had been in "safe hands" that night, the fact that she disappeared last night with an ambulance and showed up here.

She laughs. "Oh, is that what you think?"

"What the hell should I think?"

Mictlantecuhtli couldn't have appeared to Tabitha as Alex because the only connection he has right now to the outside world is me. He said he can observe, has observed, the world going on around him, but I'm the only person he can talk to. So he couldn't have appeared to her to tell her I was in that electronics store surrounded by demons.

But someone else has been keeping tabs on me. I twist the ring around my finger. It's gold now, a string of tiny *calaveras* etched in its surface. Is it always that when I see her? And jade when I see Mictlantecuhtli? I can't remember.

She sips at her coffee. I clench my fists, ready to wipe that goddamn smirk off her face. "You should think that I'd never stoop to being someone's puppet. Husband."

It doesn't register at first. Doesn't quite sink in. But when it does the room starts to spin and my feet almost give out. "Oh, Jesus."

"I'm good, aren't I? Cold, imperious Santa Muerte, the skeletal bride, and cute, perky Tabitha who can't quite adjust to this big, wide world of magic. It's easier than you might think."

I sit on the arm of the sofa, my world dropping out from under me. Bad enough that I thought she was working for her, but this? I shake myself out of it, the shock wearing off. Now's the time to get answers.

"What if I don't believe you," I say. I've been lied to a lot, lately. And some of it's been with the truth.

She says nothing, her expression doesn't change. But

then the skin on her face cracks in long fissures, strips of red meat falling away from bone as her hair drops out of her scalp in clumps. She grows taller, hands lengthening, skin falling away from spindly fingers. Soon she's a grinning skeleton, all smooth, white bone and a stink of roses and smoke. It takes forever and no time at all, a blink of an eye and an eternity.

And then she's Tabitha again, sipping her coffee.

"Convinced?" she says, putting the mug down.

"Convinced enough," I say. "Why Tabitha? Why not appear as Vivian? Or the Bruja? If you can be anyone, why Tabitha?"

"Mmm. The Bruja. I don't think she likes you much. Anyway, it's not like that. Eric, I know you better than you know yourself. You'd burned every bridge you ever had here. You wouldn't trust Vivian appearing out of nowhere. You wouldn't trust another mage. You certainly weren't going to trust Santa Muerte. No, you needed some nice, normal girl that you didn't have any history with. You needed a friend. So I gave you one."

"Is that why you killed my sister? To show that you care?"

"I'm sorry about that," she says, face growing serious.

"No, you're not."

"You're right, I'm not. Eric, to be whole Mictlan needs a queen *and* a king. One without the other and it withers. It's been withering for hundreds of years. All that time I've been searching for someone to take Mictlantecuhtli's place. And then I found you. You should be flattered. I'm trying to turn you into a god."

"You're trying to turn me into a piece of statuary to get the old king back. That's why you got Sergei to steal the knife. Yeah, I had a talk with your ex. I know how we're switching places. And you're going to kill me to bring him back."

She says nothing for a long time and then barks out a laugh. "That's what he told you? No. I don't want him back. He made his choice and he's welcome to it. He can sit in that dumpy little tomb of his and rot for all I care." She takes my hands in hers. "Eric, I chose you. You are the next king of Mictlan. Not him. I know we got off on the wrong foot—"

I pull my hands away, give her a shove. "I think murdering my sister's a bit much for 'the wrong foot,' don't you?" I pull up my shirt, show her the patch of jade in my gut. "If he's lying, explain this."

"That part he's not lying about. You are merging. But I didn't send Sergei after you." She pauses, lets that sink in. I don't know if she's telling the truth. Of course, I don't know if Mictlantecuhtli's telling me the truth, either.

"I don't think that Mictlantecuhtli intended for Sergei to try to kill you with that knife," she says. "I think he sent Sergei to give it to you so you could kill me with it. I'd thought of doing the same thing, actually. But not to kill you. To finally end him."

"So why didn't you make a play for the knife?"

"Because I trusted you would get it on your own. Eric, you're the only hope I have to make Mictlan whole. Yes, I'm using you, but not like you think. Mictlantecuhtli made his choice a long time ago. And until he's gone and someone takes his place Mictlan will fester. I need you to take the knife and kill Mictlantecuhtli. That will stop this. All of his power will be yours and he'll be gone."

"Seems dead's a hard thing to pin down with gods," I say. "You sure that would work?"

"If you took the knife and stabbed him with it hard enough he'd cease to exist. You don't get any more dead than that. He hates me, Eric. He wants me gone. Do you know how he got in that tomb? It was a mistake. He lured a bunch of Conquistadors there to kill me."

"That sounds like a piss-poor plan," I say.

"They had help," she says. "But things went wrong, and I fought. Now instead of me stuck in that tomb it's him. He wants Mictlan for himself, thinks he can hold it all together on his own, and refuses to believe that it needs both a king and a queen. He doesn't care about making it what it once was. You may not believe me, but it's not Hell. It's Paradise. At least it used to be. And it can be again."

I'm in the middle of a divine, domestic pissing match and I don't know which side to believe. It's a lot to take in. I don't trust Mictlantecuhtli and I sure as hell don't trust her. But one of them needs to be telling the truth, right? I have no idea which one of them to believe.

"So what if Mictlan goes to shit? How is that my problem?"

"Because you took me up on my offer," she says. "No take-backs. Help me, and you become a god. Do nothing, and be imprisoned for eternity as a lump of lifeless rock."

"Some choice."

"An easy choice."

"You let Sergei shoot you," I say. "Didn't you? You knew I'd try to save you and that it'd trigger these abilities."

"I wasn't planning on it," she says. "It just worked out that way. I thought it best to go along and let things play out. I wanted to see if your powers would manifest and what you might do with them. Nicely done, by the way. Using them to heal would never have occurred to Mictlantecuhtli."

"And the ambulance crew? Where are they?"

"Home, I imagine. Confused and wondering what happened last night. Once you left there wasn't any reason to keep up the charade so I left. None of them will remember a thing."

"And what about 'Tabitha'? Did she ever exist? Was she ever real?" I say.

"Yes. She died a couple of years ago."

"The car accident." When I met Tabitha she told me how she'd discovered her own small powers. Her car went over the side of the freeway one night and instead of dying in a fiery car crash her magic had manifested and saved her. Guess it didn't quite work out that way.

"She was dying, and as she breathed her last I moved in. Not all of me, a seed. This body is just an extension of me. I'm here, and in Mictlan, and in the dreams of my followers. I'm Death, Eric. I can be anywhere, any time. 'Tabitha' is an avatar. Some of me, some of her. Sometimes it's hard to tell where one ends and the other begins, to be honest."

"This is how you got past my masking spell," I say. Santa Muerte could track me down, but she couldn't see me. I was a big blind spot. But 'Tabitha' is Santa Muerte and not Santa Muerte. Human enough to fool the spell. "How you found me at the electronics store."

"It is," she says.

"Did you kill her?" I say.

She hesitates, but a moment later says, "Yes."

Rage flares in me and in a flash I grab her and yank her against me. I have the obsidian blade hard against her throat, its point dimpling her skin.

"You murdered someone who I'd never met just to use her against me. Give me one goddamn reason why I shouldn't slit your throat right now."

"Why would I stop you?" she says, her voice a hot whisper against my cheek. "Go on. Kill me. That's what that blade is for, Eric. Tear out my heart and bathe in my blood. That knife will kill this body. But the mind in it? That's only a small piece of me. A splinter of who I am. 'Tabitha' will die, but I'll be just fine. Do you want to have to explain to Vivian that you murdered her friend, her only other tie to the dead fiancé you killed? I don't think that'll go over very well, do you?"

It's tempting. So tempting. But I know it won't solve a thing. And much as I know that this is Santa Muerte in Tabitha's body and that the woman I thought she was died before I ever met her, I don't think I can kill her. She leans in closer to me, the blade nicking her neck, a thin line of blood running down her throat, and brings her lips a hairsbreadth from mine.

"Kiss me or kill me, Eric. But pick one."

I shove her away from me, opting for neither. She wipes a tear of blood from her throat with a fingertip and licks it off. The wound seals up a moment later, no sign it was ever there.

"No?" she says. "Pity." I'm not sure which one she'd prefer.

"So what now?"

She shrugs. "I walk out that door. Unless you want to stop me. I can think of a few reasons to stick around. But something tells me you need a little time to adjust before we try that again."

"I can stop you," I say, but there's no conviction in my voice.

"You can," she says. "I won't even fight you. I think I even have some duct tape and zip-ties around here somewhere. Might be fun. But what will that get you? Are you going to keep me in the closet? And what happens when Vivian comes calling? No, I'm going to leave. But we'll see each other again." She smiles, blows a kiss at me, walks out the door.

And I let her.

I wait until I hear the Mini drive away then pull out my phone. I need to call Vivian, explain to her what just happened, to not trust Tabitha or anything she says. Somehow explain that a trusted friend, the last tie she has to her dead fiancé, is not what she appears. Instead, I call someone else.

"Well? Did I call it?" Gabriela says when she picks up.

I thought I'd figured everything out on my drive over, but something wasn't sitting right. I needed another pair of eyes on this thing and I couldn't think of anyone else I could talk to about it, so I called Gabriela, even though I knew she didn't want to talk to me again. Took some fast talking to get her to not hang up, but I told her what I'd been thinking, that this wasn't over. That Tabitha was working with Santa Muerte.

Gabriela listened then told me that no, Tabitha *was* Santa Muerte.

"I owe you twenty bucks."

"Booyah," she says. "Did you kill her?"

"No. Thought about it. But she's just an avatar. Just an extension. Killing her'd just leave me a body and wouldn't solve the problem."

"You could have at least tried."

I answer that with silence.

"Okay, fine," she says. "I'm just saying you have no idea if she was telling the truth or yanking your chain. And killing her wouldn't have cost you anything. Seriously, you can't tell me you of all people don't know how to get rid of a body. So why'd you let her go?"

I don't answer for a long time. I'm not entirely sure why I didn't do it. Maybe it's because, no matter what she's done, she's still Tabitha, that I'm holding out some hope that it's not true. And then it comes to me. I turn the obsidian blade in my hands. It's a stupid idea. It will probably get me killed.

"I think I still need her," I say, the bones of a plan forming in my mind. I think about what I've heard from Santa Muerte and from Mictlantecuhtli, about what their domestic squabble has cost me, has cost my friends and family. I heft the obsidian blade in my hand. I wonder how much fire will satisfy my promise to the Santa Anas.

"For what?"

"To kill a couple of gods."

Diana Rowland

"Rowland's delightful novel jumps genre lines with a little something for everyone—mystery, horror, humor, and even a smattering of romance. Not to be missed—all that's required is a high tolerance for gray matter. For true zombiephiles, of course, that's a no brainer."

—*Library Journal*

"An intriguing mystery and a hilarious mix of the horrific and mundane...Humor and gore are balanced by surprisingly touching moments as Angel tries to turn her (un)life around."

—*Publishers Weekly*

My Life as a White Trash Zombie
978-0-7564-0675-2

Even White Trash Zombies Get the Blues
978-0-7564-0750-6

White Trash Zombie Apocalypse
978-0-7564-0803-9

How the White Trash Zombie Got Her Groove Back
978-0-7564-0822-0

To Order Call: 1-800-788-6262
www.dawbooks.com

DAW 201

Joe Sunday's dead...

...he just hasn't stopped moving yet.

Sunday's a thug, an enforcer, a leg-breaker for hire. When his boss sends him to kill a mysterious new business partner, his target strikes back in ways Sunday could never have imagined. Murdered, brought back to a twisted half-life, Sunday finds himself stuck in the middle of a race to find an ancient stone with the power to grant immortality. With it, he might live forever. Without it, he's just another rotting extra in a George Romero flick.

Everyone's got a stake, from a psycho Nazi wizard and a razor-toothed midget, to a nympho-demon bartender, a too-powerful witch who just wants to help her homeless vampires, and the one woman who might have all the answers — if only Sunday can figure out what her angle is.

Before the week is out he's going to find out just what lengths people will go to for immortality. And just how long somebody can hold a grudge.

City of the Lost
by Stephen Blackmoore
978-0-7564-702-5

DAW 209